BETWIXT TWISTS AND TURNS

BETWIXT TWISTS AND TURNS

A POTPOURRI OF SHORT STORIES

MONA MOHANTY

PARTRIDGE

To order additional copies of this book, contact
Partridge India
000 800 10062 62
orders.india@partridgepublishing.com

www.partridgepublishing.com/india

Contents

To my dearest mum.

Wish you could read this, Mummy,
And be proud of me,
For you have shaped me
Into what I am today.

Acknowledgements

This is a collection of stories born out of random thoughts popping up out of nowhere, unwittingly heard whiffs of conversation between strangers, parables from the family lore, and anecdotes from friends. Then collating them together into this medley of words and getting them to see the light of day took a lot of prodding from my family and close friends. I can never forget the encouragement proffered by various people directly or indirectly connected with me.

My beloved parents, Mr Chandidas Mohanty and Mrs Rashmi Mohanty, constantly nurtured and fed my voracious appetite for letters and the written word. My delightful siblings, Dimpy and Dev, spurred me on with their loving irreverence. My darling boys, Tanmay and Aman (I dare not mention their nicknames here!), never believed—and still don't—that their Mum possessed a serious (read writer) side. But, that did not stop them from trying to surreptitiously peek into my penned thoughts.

My friends from school (and there are many!)—specifically those from St Joseph's High School (Bhubaneswar), La Martiniere Girls' College (Lucknow), and the Frank Anthony Public School (New Delhi)—and my pals from Lady Shri Ram College for Women and the Jawaharlal University (New Delhi) were constantly enquiring when this would see the light of day. So, friends, here it is finally!

My colleagues in the Indian Revenue Service as well as close friends in other civil services have always believed in me, and I am indebted to them for the same. I do have the 'right' kinda friends.

Last but not the least, this offering will not be complete if I do not mention my friends in social media, my dear Facebook and WhatsApp friends. I can actually never thank them enough for kindling my creativity.

Whoops, my list hasn't ended. To the production team at Penguin Partridge Publications comprising of the lovely ladies, Marge, Emily, Gemma and Mary, a big thank you for helping me meet my deadlines through your gentle reminders.

1

Wandering

Waking up at five o'clock in the morning was not such a big deal! *One could ask the oldies,* she thought, for when she did get out of bed and switch on the lights (it was still dark at that hour in the month of November in Delhi), she saw that quite a few of the ancients had beaten her to it. She espied some lights in the distance; she called them ancient because none of the youngsters or those in the middle-aged bracket got up so early unless it was for herding off children to school, college, etc.

However, dear reader, lest you think that she too was bordering on ancient, she most certainly was no dowager. It was just that she liked getting up at an hour before the routine and stress of reality—in other words, before real life set in. Carrying a huge mug of tea, her one and only indulgence, she sauntered on to the balcony. It was yet to be light. Even the birds were asleep! The sky would by and by get lighter. The stillness and its very soothing silence calmed the mind further, letting it career across the path of daydreams, or was it a night dream?

Like a somnambulist, she explored the tunnel of life: the unencumbered freedom of childhood; the lack of responsibility; catching butterflies and letting them go (just for the momentary pleasure of having a living being under her control); climbing mango trees in the neighbours' yard on a hot, sleepy afternoon, then getting caught and being soundly thrashed by her parent (at that time, there was nothing dictatorial about such actions, nor did she feel that it was undeserved); passing over the unappetizing titbits on the plate to an ever-willing and perennially hungry dog who happened to be her pet.

She remembered the trips to the zoo, where she wept at the sight of the lonesome but beautiful animals in their cages and asked her mother to be allowed to take them home. Her mind veered towards the childhood game of hopscotch, the expected and interminable quarrels among her peers amidst accusations of cheating, the tears, and pummelling one another with fists and then making up. She recalled curling up on a wet day with her favourite Enid Blyton book or Phantom comics with the smell of baking wafting in from the kitchen.

Suddenly, her thoughts were interrupted by a short sharp sound like a squeak. Craning her head in that direction, she saw two eyes peering at her from the balcony wall as she sat without moving a muscle. It was a face-off to check out who would blink first. There was another squeak, and then the squirrel eyed her tea, pondered for a few seconds, and as if coming to a momentous decision, vanished without as much as a by-your-leave. Her thoughts at that moment were that of trying to place herself in the mind of the animal.

What thoughts had passed in its mind? she wondered. Was it overwhelmed by what would have been to her, relatively speaking, massive proportions as compared to its tiny visage? Or did her tea remind it of its need to forage for food? Maybe its tummy had rumbled! She had never had a squirrel looking at her just a few inches away from her face.

She stretched and leaned over the balcony and saw signs of life picking up; the sky was now over yellowish pink, the crows cawed, and a few parrots twittered over the top of a gulmohar tree. She could see a few ladies venturing out to pick the yellow and white flowers for the morning puja(worship).

Tring went the doorbell. It was the maid, followed a few minutes later by the newspaper delivery. As was the pattern of lawlessness pervading all aspects of life, the newspaper contained news of financial scams, embezzlement, political brouhaha, murder, and gore. It was as if nothing nice happened any more. As if an unseen signal had switched them on, the mobiles started ringing, and the computers got switched on even before the mandatory routine of brushing teeth. It was a proclamation of a new world that was unfolding by wiping out the old natural one.

Turning to get back to her morning chores, she was arrested by the sight of a swarm of dragonflies! She looked up, scanning the sky for approaching clouds, for didn't the old-timers say that dragonflies flying around were harbingers of rain!

The doorbell rang again. *Tch, who can it be right now?* she thought irritably as she went to answer the door. It was the postman with the 'dreaded' missive—the telegram. With fumbling fingers, she tore it open, and the contents were the usual sanitized sentences: 'With deep regret, we inform you that your husband died fighting bravely in the line of duty.'

As the scrap of paper floated down from her nerveless fingers, she felt herself falling into a dark abyss. All she could think of was that the dragonflies were the messengers of much more than rain.

2

In the Mind's Eye

My rheumy and not-so-bright eyes had seen them all—happiness, sorrow, anger, jealousy, bitterness, success—and the juxtaposition of the myriad emotions that constitute life.

When one grows to a ripe old age, as in my case, little things like warts on the skin cease to be a bother. For life is like a river, gushing at its source, torpedoing down mountains, meandering through valleys, and gurgling along plains (at times, calm; at others, turbulent) before finally merging with the sea. Following the riverine pattern, life begins with a roar (literally!), moving through infancy, running along childhood, catapulting into adolescence, maturing into sedate adulthood, and sliding into old age.

And this arrangement was no different in the neighbourhood that I dwelt in. It consisted of a motley group of individuals as disparate as they could be, for they spanned all ages, colour, and creed and originated from various walks of life.

Interesting families were like that of the doctor couple; the beautiful young wife wept copious tears at her charming husband's infidelity. Then there was the fat family-excluding one (for the father was reed thin); it was difficult to distinguish the mother and the daughter because they, with their gargantuan proportions, looked exactly the same from a distance. Then there was the plain bespectacled girl who accompanied her beautiful friend whenever the latter met her boyfriend—ostensibly to divert the mother's attention from the fact of her daughter's amorous sojourn.

And of course, as in any neighbourhood in any town or city of India, there were the wastrels hanging around and singing ribald songs at the crossroad whenever a personable girl walked by. How could one forget the right royal fracas when the old retired schoolteacher picked up his cane to ward off berry-stealing youngsters from his garden or the shrill-voiced grandma who shooed away the smack-addicted ragpicker in a not-so-gentle manner?

Well, that was the general scene of a typical neighbourhood in any street in any area of any town or city in India, and I thought I had seen it all. I was about to turn and get back to what I had been doing when I clearly heard the sound of sobbing. I froze, for my ears registered the choked gasps of someone struggling to stop her emotions from spilling over—yes, she was speaking to someone, albeit in a low tone.

Oh, maybe a lover's tiff, I thought as I turned away. But then came a sudden shriek which pierced the innards of my heart—it was unearthly—like the last song of a dying swan. Before I could gather my wits around me, there was a resounding splash.

I leapt aside, for I was just a frog in the well.

3

A Drive

It had been a strange drive. The day dawned sunny and bright to begin with as we negotiated our way through bustling traffic across the length and breadth of the city. It was eight o'clock in the morning, and it seemed as if three-quarters of the population was out on the streets. I had a feeling that the census figures were way off the mark in what they reported. How did the earth withstand the combined weight of man, animal, machinery, equipment, and transport! The once-beautiful city looked as if it was about to burst at its seams. No wonder tempers rode so high; the pressure on the existing infrastructure was unbelievable.

Anyway, I was glad to get out of the city. My journey was to a town sixty kilometres away; it wasn't my usual job, but I was filling in for a colleague who was ill, and there were certain urgent documents to be signed by the client. As we turned on to the highway, which was miraculously and remarkably uncluttered by traffic, I gradually drifted into somnolence. I slept on, oblivious of the sounds and sights of the countryside that we were traversing through. The blaring of the horn woke me up a few minutes before we were due to enter the municipal limits of the town. Rubbing my sleep-infested eyes, I craned my neck forward to see the cause of the cacophony and stifled a laugh. It was just an errant bullock who had decided to plonk himself in the middle of the highway, the master of all that he surveyed. Vehicles of myriad hues, shapes, and sizes skirted around him.

While we veered on one side to go ahead, the car suddenly stalled and sputtered to a halt. *Oh heavens,* I thought as I suddenly noticed the ominous clouds in the horizon. In the next minute, hailstones pelted the roof, and then all of a sudden, the downpour ended as quickly as it had begun. The sun was out. If one did not look at the countryside too closely to view the dampness and register the faint smell of mud, I would have thought that I was dreaming.

I sauntered out of the car and walked on ahead to a roadside dhaba(eatery) while the driver tinkered with the car. It was a quaint dhaba, brightly painted and decorated with colourful streamers and manned by a wizened old man who was cheerfully brewing tea. While making small talk, he mentioned that he had been running the place for the past sixty years and drove down every day from his village, fifteen kilometres in the interior. He had a red Maruti van in tip-top condition parked under a tree.

Nursing a delicious cup of masala chai(spice flavoured tea), I listened to him rambling with my eyes looking at my watch and the driver simultaneously. It was getting late. However, in spite of my protestations, the dhaba owner plied me with stuffed parathas(fried unleavened bread) with generous dollops of butter over them. He shook his head knowingly and muttered that the younger generation (presumably, I was part of it) did not appreciate good, healthy home-cooked food. I chuckled inwardly while the thought of my diet going for a six flitted through my mind.

Finally, the driver beckoned to me. I paid my bill and left. As I approached the town, I saw fire tenders and an ambulance. The driver came back, ashen-faced, with the news that the newly constructed flyover leading into the town had collapsed twenty minutes back and at least ten cars had gone along with it. The prognosis about the fate of the occupants was not good.

Gosh, we could have been on it, I thought, *if the break down had not happened.*

I called the client and gave him news of the collapse. Very solicitous, he asked me if I was all right and asked me to return and that we could meet after things had settled down.

My colleague was down with a bout of viral fever and, hence, out of action for a fortnight as per the doctor's orders. So it was my job to meet the client for the next briefing.

This time, the client came to our office. After the meeting was concluded to the mutual satisfaction of both sides, we went out for lunch. While waiting for our food, I asked him whether the flyover had been restored.

He told me that it would require a lot of time to complete it because it had to be built ab initio. At the moment, a bypass had been created for travellers. I asked him if it would affect the old man's dhaba business.

Puzzled, he looked at me and asked, 'Which dhaba?'

I told him about the old man, his dhaba, and the red car. I also mentioned the fact about our car breaking down near it and how the delay had proved providential.

My client was silent. I wondered at his confusion. There was nothing else in that area but the dhaba! Very quietly, breaking the uncomfortable silence that had followed my words, he said that the dhaba I had been speaking of had been burnt down along with its owner and his car twenty years back by miscreants who had sought to rob it.

You could have heard a pin drop!

4

A Meeting

'Sheela? Oh, Sheela, where are you? This woman,' muttered Avinash as he looked for his pen drive, 'why doesn't she turn up when required!' Slowly his temper—which, even at the best of times, hovered just below the surface of the sophisticated veneer that he presented to the world— reached the rim of the burning cauldron and erupted.

With one sweep of his arm, he swept away all the bottles and jars on his wife's dressing table. A sickeningly gooey mess created splashes on the floor; pink and white blobs of cream and shimmering glitter of eyeshadow amidst shades of glass cut rainbow-like streaks of sunlight that sliced through the windowpanes, and above it all was the overwhelming smell of the amalgamation of perfumes.

Sheela stood trembling outside the door and was wondering at her latest fault. Most of the time, she was beaten up without even knowing the reason for it. For instance, yesterday, it was—as conveyed to her in soul-shivering tones two hours after being kicked around mercilessly on the floor—because she had exceeded the regular quota of five minutes per week allowed to her for speaking with her mother over the phone. No allowances were made for the fact that her father was hospitalized and in a serious condition. Of course, there was no question of visiting them. After all, what would her brother and his wife be doing otherwise?

At a glance, she took in the mess in her room, and before she could open her mouth, her furious husband picked up his overnight travel bag and rushed out without even looking at her. Obviously, he was in a hurry, and that saved her from his ire at that moment. She followed him at a safe distance and saw him get into the cab and get driven away.

God, at least a day's relief, if not more, she thought, hoping that if he had gone out of town, maybe he would stay back for a couple of days.

Avinash, on the way to the airport, showered abuses on the driver for driving slowly as it was apparent that he was going to make it just in the nick of time. The driver, with his earphones on, was oblivious to his passenger's fury till he was tapped on the shoulders. Taking off his earplugs, he told his irate passenger that he was driving at the maximum speed limit possible and that he did not (he said with a smirk) intend breaking the law. But if he had an issue with his driving, he was free to take another cab.

Simmering silently for he had no other choice, Avinash leaned back and looked at the ornate watch that he flaunted for business meetings. The trees breezed by, drivers honked, pedestrians on the sidewalk strode purposefully towards their destination, and it was bright and sunny with not a cloud in the sky. In all, it was a beautiful day. But he noticed none of these as the drive went on endlessly.

Finally, the grey outlines of the airport loomed large. Having paid the cab driver beforehand, on the figure agreed upon before hopping onto it, he rushed out even before the car had come to a standstill. The cabbie drove away, shaking his head. 'Why don't they call us earlier if they need to reach on time?' he muttered.

He was glad that he had reached with five minutes to spare. Purposefully, he strode to the check-in counter, pasting a perfunctory smile on his face as he presented his ticket to the lady manning it.

'Sorry, sir, you cannot board this flight,' she was saying, 'because it is overbooked.'

'But', he stuttered, 'I have an urgent meeting in three hours' time.'

'I am sorry, sir,' she said, hardly looking contrite, 'but we have already offloaded five passengers. I suggest that you take the next flight out in the evening.'

'Do you realize', he ranted, 'that my meeting is with someone who is flying back to the US in five hours? I am going to sue the airline for this.'

Hearing the commotion, a suitably and seriously attired (dark suit and all), bespectacled young man smoothly glided up to him and said that he would arrange a business class ticket at economy rates in the next flight to make up for this inconvenience. Pushing him away, Avinash stormed away from the counter. He called up his client, who brusquely informed him that the deal between them was off.

Avinash pleaded with him to extend his stay by a day, but the person at the other end was unmoved, saying that Avinash needed to prioritize his affairs. The prospective client disconnected the phone but not before adding that they didn't need him as much as he needed them. Staggering at the blow, he moved out of the airport towards the line of cabs. Dialling home, he heard Sheela pick up the phone at the first ring.

'Hello,' she said in a trembling voice.

'You bitch, you made me miss my flight. Today I'll fix you and—aaaah!'

There was a squeal of brakes and an ear-splitting shriek. Through the receiver, she heard voices in the background.

'Oh my god!'

'Feel his pulse.'

'Chase the car.'

'Did you note the number?'

'Poor guy, no pulse . . .'

'Make way, I am a doctor.'

'Call the ambulance.'

'No use, he is dead. Inform the family.'

'This mobile flew out of his hand. Hello, who is on the line?'

Sheela said, 'I am Sheela. What happened? This is my husband's mobile. Where is he?'

'I am sorry, ma'am,' said the voice. 'There has been an accident. He is no more.'

For the first time in five years, Sheela laughed and laughed and laughed.

5

Turning the Corner

Oh god! Where on earth was the curtain? Goodness, did they have to wash them again that day? But first things first! He had to escape from that monster. Oh great, the washroom door was ajar.

Cowering down on all fours, he stealthily entered the darkly comforting sanctuary of the tiny space, the merits of which he had not appreciated until now. It was nice and cool, given the fact that there was no sunlight on this side of the property. Slowly, some of the tension left his body, and as relaxation set in, he felt his eyelids grow heavy as he dozed off into a languorous slumber.

The crashing of the door awakened him from a soporifically exotic dream where he was the centre of attraction, being fed all the goodies that he longed for, like a comfortable mattress (soft and with downy cover), and having no one to bully him by brute force.

In his view, just the fact that he was a tiny being, albeit advanced in years, did not grant licence to the occupants of this house to torture him. The head of the household was the least of his worries, for he left for work early in the morning; it was his wife and her obnoxious son who were the main culprits in the torture chamber.

Madam, who responded to the silly name Buttercup, usually had her loud and crass girlfriends over for at least four days in a week, and then it was a babble of voices, high-pitched screeches (bad for his heart, he averred), and zero-calorie diet food which was singularly unappetizing that even he, who remained perennially hungry, did not salivate. Those days were the pits, with him being relegated to that corner of the house and the help telling him, in a hushed whisper, not to be seen or heard. What was the point in the idiot opening his mouth when he invariably turned the key in the door after he left? And as usual, the scoundrel left no water for him even in times of soaring temperatures.

Then the boy, Arjun, with his pot belly would come and poke him in the ribs and try to smother him with his pudgy fists. At times, if no one was looking, he would even drop hot milk on his bed. Was there ever going to be a reprieve!

Mister Ravi was in a real temper today. Ravi was the head of the family! Even the spouse and the carrier of the lineage were uncharacteristically mousy. Ravi muttered, 'Why on earth is she coming? I have some important meetings lined up today.'

His ears perked up! Who was coming? Buttercup was getting some special food cooked in the kitchen, and all minions were on the job. The house had never been so spick and span. It actually smelt good for a change.

The bell rang. The family stood at attention as the door opened. Oh my god, such a regal-looking lady. Ravi touched her feet, and so did his 'attachments', the wife and the son. The lady hugged them.

Without wasting any time on preliminaries and trying to, in a discreet manner, probe his grandma about her itinerary, Ravi said, 'Dadi, this is a pleasant surprise. You have come back after many years.'

Grandma said, 'Son, I have come here to stay here permanently, for life abroad can be really lonesome. Your cousin and his wife are out all day at their workplaces, and there is no social interaction with neighbours. They live in the suburbs, and the nearest neighbour lives a mile away. Here, at least, I shall have the company of your wife and son.'

The resident members of the family were uncharacteristically quiet at dinner. Post dinner, Grandma wanted to see the house. She was taken on a tour. He heard them walking past his door and then suddenly he heard firm steps and the door opened. With the light streaming in behind her, Grandma walked in, and that was the day when he was relocated from his room to Dadi's room.

He slept with her now, the sleep of the totally fulfilled. No more hunger pangs, no discomfort or meddlesome kid, and all because Dadi was rich, obscenely so. Ravi, the grandson, was the one of only two heirs, and Dadi could not stand the sight of a dog on a leash and tied up in a corner and tortured as he was!

Perish the thought! Moneytalks.

It was a dog's life, and he was not complaining!

6

Life's a Well

Neeti was woken up in the middle of the night by her usual nightmare. Wiping off the beads of perspiration from her brow, she got up from her *chatai* (floor mat), manoeuvred her way around the supine figure on the floor, and tiptoed across the courtyard to the kitchen. It was a moonlit night and absolutely quiet. Gulping down two glasses of water, she calmed her hyper-stretched nerves and, mopping her brow, gingerly made her way back to her mattress without a sound.

'Alok, where are you?' she whispered as she wept silently with muffled sobs into her pillow. Her childhood playmate and companion, whom she had unabashedly laughed with, ferociously fought with, and even cried with at times of sorrow was the man she had known and loved, whom she would have wed. Why had he done this to her? Their romance had been the stuff of dreams and envy of the people around them.

She still remembered seeing him off at the bus stand as he went off to the city to pursue a professional course. She would wait at the same place whenever he came back on vacation. The years passed by, and he got a job. On his last trip back to town, he had said that he would ask his parents to speak to hers for their marriage on his next visit home. The day of his proposed visit came and went. She waited till evening, watching each bus that came from town discharge its passengers, but none of them was her beloved. Despite her frantic calls, his cell phone continued to give the 'switched off' message.

Finally, after two days, in desperation, she went to his house in the neighbouring village. His mother opened the door. Greeting her by touching her feet, she stood up after obtaining her blessing and asked her why Alok hadn't come and if his number had changed. His father, who had been in the background, had, on seeing her, gone in abruptly after nodding at her greeting.

Watching her husband's retreating back with a strained expression and with tears in her eyes, his mother told her that Alok had met with an accident and that he was no more. She said that she didn't know how to break this news to her, and hence, they had kept silent.

Neeti slowly walked back all the ten kilometres back to her village, totally numb. On her way back, she crossed the well, that very well where she had met Alok so many times. How could he have left her like this? Standing near the edge, watching the swaying rope on which the bucket was hung, she looked deep into the water; she saw her reflection and, behind her, another man—Alok.

Oh, praise the Lord, for it dawned on her instantly that he was alive. Her face lit up and then came a thought. Why on earth had his mother said that he was dead? Oh, okay, it must have been Alok's way of playing a prank. But this time, she felt that he had carried things a little too far. Slowly, she felt her anger boil over as she turned towards him. At that precise moment, her friend Kamla, who was working in the fields nearby, stumbled, fell, and screamed in agony.

Alok, I'll not forgive you for this, she thought as she rushed to help Kamla. After checking for any serious injuries and satisfied that there were none, she got Kamla to hobble to the safety of her home. But by the time she returned to the well, Alok had disappeared.

The least he could have done, she thought crossly, *was to wait for me.*

When she reached home, her mother, with her face wreathed in a huge smile, hugged her and said, 'My dear daughter, finally, you shall have happiness. Your grandpa has fixed your marriage, and both the boy's parents and he like you.'

Perplexed she asked, 'Who?'

Her mother said, 'Your would-be husband is Alok.'

So he was here, she thought. Finally, her parents now knew of her and Alok unlike his parents, who had been aware of their relationship.

Blushing, she asked her mother with a smile, 'Where is he?'

Sternly, her dadi said, 'You are not to talk, speak, or meet with him till the wedding is over. No newfangled practices can interfere with time-bound customs.' She tempered her harshness by pulling at her cheek lovingly.

*   *   *

Neeti, a radiant bride, was seen off with her new husband on the way to her marital home. The car sped through the village and on to the highway.

Oh, he is taking me to his house in town and not in the village, she thought.

Alok did not speak, and try as much as she could to sneak a peak, his face was not visible through her heavy veil. Even during the marriage ceremony, she had not been able to catch a glimpse of him because of the flowers covering his face. Maybe he was quiet because of the relatives sitting in front. So she too sat quietly while her excitement simmered.

After a five-hour drive, they reached her husband's home, where a strange lady welcomed her in the traditional manner of heralding the arrival of a new bride.

Where is Alok's mother? she thought.

After hours of being shown off to relatives and friends, she was finally taken to the bridal chamber, her husband's room—no, their room! Amidst high-pitched giggles and suggestive nudges, the girls escorting her left the room when her husband walked in.

Gently, he lifted her veil and said that he had fallen in love with her the day he had come to her village on work and seen her at the well. What was wrong with his voice? She lifted her eyes. It was the face of a stranger. Tears welled up in her eyes, for this stranger was not her Alok.

The well threw up a bride's body the next day.

7

Wind beneath My Wings

Oof! I hated these early morning flights. I never was a morning person. No, I did not want to hear the cock crow or see the streaks of various shades of red, orange, and yellow light up the sky or feel the dew on the grass under my feet. I did not like hearing the thud of the newspaper hitting my balcony door. Also, I did not like hearing the sounds of the pressure cooker whistling away next door at the neighbour's. Moreover, I did not like smelling the fresh and cool early morning jogger's air or seeing the dogs leading their masters for their daily constitutional. I did not like the sounds of school buses honking while they wait to pick up their 'usually' reluctant passengers or of the television sets blaring away with morning bhajans. I was not a morning person. Period!

I preferred the blinds drawn tightly, no sounds of early morning activity penetrating my consciousness while I slept the dreamless sleep of the, er, innocent. Morning should seep in very slowly into the subconscious, taking its own sweet meandering course, penetrating the layers of sleep cushioning the senses. As I wove out of slumber, my senses came alive, my eyes half-closed, my nostrils sniffing for the lingering aroma of strong coffee (for nothing on earth is as delicious to wake up to), and I allowed my limbs to stretch to their fullest and soak in the vibrancy of life.

But none of that luxury was meant for me this morning. I had a flight to catch to Dehradun, for the all-important client had hysterically insisted on my presence at 9 a.m. in his office. A hush-hush merger bid was taking place, and he was paranoid about coming to our offices, so who would be the proverbial lamb sent for slaughter if not yours truly? Poor, unsuspecting me! For I had been fattened up before the lightning bolt struck and found its mark—with frothy, strong coffee and potato crispies at teatime yesterday. It did not take much to lead me into a state of euphoric blunderbuss!

Anyway, here I was at the airport, totally aggrieved and displeased with my lot in life. *The bright lights of the airport and the incredibly crowded counters—how and why do people travel at this unearthly hour?* I thought. Rubbing my bleary eyes, I stared morosely at a group of giggling girls. How could they summon so much energy in the middle of the night! For me, 5 a.m. was most certainly night.

The charms of the girl issuing the boarding pass were totally lost on me as she wished me a happy journey. I glared at her silently as I trudged away for security check. The check took its own sweet time, with the staff cracking jokes as stale as the tobacco they were chewing.

Finally, boarding was announced. As we walked towards the aircraft, I saw with a pang that it was a twenty-seater. Gosh, it would be really cramped. There was just one entry at the rear, and the stairs looked like a rope ladder. Gingerly, I made my way up, carrying my overnight bag, which thankfully fitted into the tiny cabin hold.

The saving grace was the window seat in one of the front rows. I hated aisle seats where people brushed past me on their mandatory trips to the lavatory. Even on a flight not spanning more than forty-five minutes, people did not appear to be able to control certain bodily functions.

Slowly, the aircraft filled up, the air hostess, with her polite smile, greeting all passengers as bags were fitted in either under the seat or pushed into the baggage hold above. A profusely sweating gentleman sat down in the seat next to mine. Being in no mood for small talk, I pretended to be busy with switching off my mobile and scrimmaging through my bag as if I was searching for something. But I guess I thought too much about my capacity to attract co-passengers, for the man did not say a word to me or even look towards me. The air hostess came and asked him if he was comfortable. The reply was a curt yes and an uncomfortable pause, after which she walked away.

What a rude man. The lady was merely being solicitous towards him. In fact, the sweaty visage of the gentleman had probably led her to be extra considerate. Then came the announcement by the pilot that we were ready to depart. Immediately, the plane started taxiing down the runway. As we moved ahead, the plane jolting and bustling down the runway as it gathered speed, for it was a smaller aircraft; it shook us like a sack of potatoes. Mr Sweaty was still sweating.

Finally, we were in the air, and as I looked down at the ground getting further and further away, I heard the gentleman ask the hostess for a glass of water. He gulped down not one but four glasses. Boy, he was really thirsty! I took out my novel and started reading.

The man was really fidgety. First, he unbuckled his belt once he was allowed to do so. He stretched his body at an awkward angle, almost reclining three-fourths of his length sideways. He repeated this action twice, turning on both sides and then sat up and scanned the safety manuals.

I continued reading when, suddenly, I saw him looking with bulging eyes past me through the window at the propellers of the aircraft. It was a strange feeling. His nose could have touched my cheek at the first turbulence. Before I could glare at him, he did an about turn and looked with horrified fascination through the window on the opposite side.

Oh, I thought with sympathy, *one of those frightened travellers.* I bent to ask him if he was all right, but as I was about to open my mouth, the plane suddenly banked left and remained stationary for maybe a couple of seconds. All conversation in the aircraft came to a standstill. However, the aircraft moved on its path soon after and normalcy reigned again. Before we knew it, the pilot had announced that we were descending. My co-passenger suddenly seemed to calm down a bit and started mumbling to himself. I did not want to disturb him at his prayers.

The landing was uneventful. As we passed through the airport lounge, I suddenly saw the flight attendant approach my neighbour in the plane while we were heading for our baggage. I did not mean to but could not help eavesdropping on their conversation. And I shouldn't have!

Horrified, I walked on like a zombie after I heard him saying, 'No, dear, I am just suffering from jet lag. After all, piloting a thirteen-hour transatlantic flight does take its toll. I am commanding this flight tomorrow from out of here as there is a shortage of pilots this week. Lack of sleep affects my concentration. I do hope that I manage a couple of hours of sleep tonight.'

My flight outwards had been booked for the morrow.

8

Food for Thought

It was the usual muggy morning as he cycled off to work, the picture of a man burdened by the unending responsibilities that life had bestowed upon him. He was just one of the innumerable minions trudging to work in order to earn a living. He was just twenty-eight years old but looked at least twenty years older—haggard, careworn, dripping with sweat, and even his hair had started greying. Glancing constantly at the time on his mobile, he cycled even harder, unmindful of the numerous potholes on the way.

Within a few minutes, he reached his destination, the place where numerous sounds emanated—sounds of the clinking of metal on metal, the clang of a cement mixer, the rumbling of a bulldozer, and the humming of a giant chainsaw. Slowly raising his already tired eyes, with the sun already traversing steadily overhead, he looked at the tract of land before him where numerous multistorey buildings were being constructed. That particular site had become his second home, and it felt as if he had been stationed there for years.

Three months back, having lost his earlier job, he had been having a traumatic time looking for work. Jobs, especially for accountants like him, were scarce and aspirants too many. One day, finally, it got to him. Having aged, helpless parents and a nagging wife to look after and no money to make ends meet, he had walked aimlessly on to the main road leading to the centre of the town and straight into the bonnet of a vehicle which had suddenly moved out of the adjoining petrol pump ahead.

Gesticulating, the driver got out and started raving and ranting at careless jaywalkers like him who gave a bad name to industrious citizens. Shaking his arm and not eliciting any response from him, the irate driver suddenly stopped and looked at him closely. A look of concern replaced the anger on his face. He asked him if there was something wrong. At that, he—the poor, tired soul that he was—suddenly burst into tears.

That had been, amidst all that confusion, a day which had turned the tide and his fortunes. For the man who had stopped to scold him had been an executive in a business group engaged in real estate activities. He found a job as a bookkeeper-cum-clerk in a construction company and was posted at the construction site's office. Life was suddenly sunnier than it had been until then.

He remembered the times when he had spent the entire day without having a morsel to swallow and the constant nagging pain in his stomach due to hunger. His wife constantly taunted him for not being man enough to handle his household affairs. She rued the day that she had stepped into his house and complained about having to be constantly tied down with the job of looking after her aged in-laws.

In fact, she had, one fine day, stopped giving him his lunch, saying that she could not be bothered to get up in the morning to cook for him and that he could pack it himself. Well, all that was in the past as he opened his tiffin box and peered into the containers.

Oh good! Rice and mutton curry again. Delicious. I have been having mutton curry continuously in the past one week, he thought. *Time to turn vegetarian.* Feeling contented, he chucked the chewed-up bone back into the container. There was a clink as the silver toe ring slipped out of the bone.

He smiled and rubbed his stomach in satisfaction.

9

Toy Stories

Remember the movie *Sleepy Hollow*? It was dark, placid, even-toned, and one got the feeling that something was going to happen any moment. Shalini, an avid movie buff, also believed that movies echoed reality. So when she moved into Arjanpur, a sleepy town as far removed from the metro she had been brought up in prior to her marriage, her mind experienced a tinge of unease the moment the vehicle carrying her, her husband, Sunil, their two year-old-daughter, Saloni, entered the street that housed their abode, which was going to be their residence till such time as Sunil's company kept him in Arjanpur.

The sky was clear, although the trees lining the road in front of the bungalow shielded the inhabitants of the houses on the street from the overhead glare of the sun. It was a quiet Sunday afternoon. People relaxed indoors in the hope that the weekend would stretch on as much as it could. Even then, she could not shake off a sense of unease.

The place is too calm, she thought.

Life soon settled down into a regular pattern. On any given working day, Sunil would get ready for office in the morning, and Saloni would have been bathed and fed. She was lucky to have her faithful maid, who had been there with her since her marriage. The day was spent in planning for the meals ahead. The dog, Rufus, an adorable Labrador, was to be taken out for his daily constitutional. The help around the house—that is, the gardener and the cook—had to be given instructions. Before she knew it, it would be lunch time.

It was only after the baby had been fed and put to bed for an afternoon nap that she found time to pursue her hobby of working on her latest embroidery project. She was adept at the art of needlework and turned out exquisite pieces which were much sought-after by her circle of friends in and around her parent's place of residence at Delhi. The popularity of her designs had germinated the idea of marketing her wares through the medium of e-retailing. But for that, she needed to bring some sort of order in her multitasking schedule. Maybe she could engage a governess for the baby after discussing it with Sunil.

Her evening schedule also followed a set pattern. Before Sunil came home, she usually took Saloni for a stroll in the park nearby. She had already made friends with young housewives living nearby—some with small children, some in the family way, and some who were either not inclined in having any or were not in a hurry to do so. It was a nice change, exchanging notes and laughing away merrily with all of them.

Two of them, Aditi and Seema, were particularly friendly. Aditi had a six-month-old son, and Seema had none. Most evenings, they walked around the path alongside the boundary walls of their houses, discussing a myriad of things as only women could do.

It was a Monday morning. Madhuri, her maid, opened the door on hearing the doorbell, presuming that it was the *doodhwala*(milkman). Shalini heard her shriek. Just in front of their door lay a doll dressed in a beautiful lacy frock, but the face on the toy, the face that had caused Madhuri to shriek, was baby Saloni's. Sunil, who had yet not left for the office, picked up the doll and, along with Shalini and the baby, drove down to the police station immediately.

At the thana, the station-in-charge took one look at the doll and said, 'Oh no, not again!' Then seeing the bewilderment on their faces, he sought to explain that almost a year back, there had been cases of six girls in the vicinity who had been reported missing from their houses, with a space of two months between each vanishing.

What was inexplicable was that these were all infants—specifically, girls—who were not more than two years old. And in each case, the episode of disappearance had been preceded by a doll with a face bearing a marked resemblance to the missing child, being left at their doorstep.

He assured them that there would be a constant watch on their residence and advised them to ensure that the baby was not left unattended at any time. A month passed, and there had been no report or evidence of any suspicious activity near their residence. Since Sunil had forbidden her to take the child out, her friends had started visiting her in the afternoon.

One day, the maid was down with fever, and Sunil was out of town, having driven down to a satellite city abutting theirs, attending to company affairs. The cook was making lunch, and the gardener had gone to his village. So Shalini picked up the baby, put her in the pram, and ventured out of the house to go down to the chemist. At the gate, she waved off the guard who wanted to accompany her, saying that she would be back in five minutes. Having got the medicine, she foraged in her purse in order to tender the exact change. She paid the pharmacist and turned to go back home and saw that the pram, with Saloni within it, had vanished. She fainted.

Coming to her senses, she found herself in her bed with a distraught Sunil who had driven back immediately after being informed of the incident, and the station-in-charge by her side. She gave an account of her movements, and sobbing continuously, she wondered how the child had not made a sound as she had been awake then.

The news spread rapidly, and both Aditi and Seema came to visit her. She was in a daze and barely listened to their commiseration. Her parents and in-laws reached their place and remained by her side constantly. Ten days passed, and still there was no news. Slowly the stream of visitors too trickled away. Aditi had to appear for her end-of-semester law examinations, and Seema called to say that her sister was ill and she had to go to Allahabad.

The next day's newspaper carried a report of a horrific train accident, the same train carrying Seema to Allahabad. There were reports of major casualties. Shaken, she rang up Seema's husband, Anil, on the phone to enquire about her. Anil seemed a little perplexed at her queries and said that Seema was at home. He then handed the phone to her.

Seema came on the line and, with a strained laugh, said that she had a lucky escape because her mother had called to inform them that her sister was better and that it had been a minor scare as she had fainted due to low blood pressure. Saying that she was fixing Anil's breakfast and that she would talk to her later, Seema abruptly put the phone down.

Around three o'clock in the afternoon, the quiet was pierced by the shrill ringing of the phone bell. It was the SHO from the police station, who said that he was on the way to their home with the baby. She interrupted him and said that she did not want to wait but would reach the police station herself. There was a short silence, and then he asked her to come to an address that he spelt out.

'Oh, but isn't that Seema's home?' she asked.

'Yes, it is,' he said and disconnected the phone.

As she rushed, innumerable queries flitting through her mind, to the given address, an ambulance taking someone to the hospital passed her with its sirens on at full blast. The SHO stood at the gate with baby Saloni. With tears flowing down her cheeks and a lump in her throat, she took her baby and, amidst sobs, thanked the cop. It was a happy reunion.

There was a constant stream of visitors and well-wishers visiting them that evening and praising the police for their quick action.

The next day, there was a news item tucked away in a corner of the local newspaper mentioning the fact that a woman, apparently unhinged, had committed suicide in their locality. Although unnamed, it was Seema. The visiting neighbours had told her that she had shot herself.

The shattered husband had no idea that the basement of the house held such awful secrets—six skeletons, baby frocks, and a diary mentioning mantras to be read on a night with a full moon before sacrificing seven infant girls in order to be blessed with a child.

Purnima was two days away!

10

The Sentinel

Auntie Rajni was taking a stroll around the park when I bumped into her on the way back from office.

She stopped right in front of me and said, 'Hello, beta, how are you? Come over, I will give you a cup of tea.'

I was exhausted after a day of interminable meetings, but the sight of that lined, aged, and smiling face made my tiredness fly away in an instant. Perking up, I replied cheerfully, 'Not today, Auntie, because I have an office party to attend, and you know how it is! Totally unavoidable!

My colleagues are coming to pick me up in half an hour because the wretched party is at a farmhouse twenty miles out of town.'

Auntie laughed that tinkling laugh of hers and said, 'Oh, you silly girl, get on with you! You don't have to apologize. Run along. We'll have tea some other day.'

Waving my hand in farewell, I rushed ahead. The next half hour passed by in a blur; my colleagues picked me up at the appointed time, and we travelled across the length of city to our destination. Amidst the slow and crawling traffic, the smog, the honking of vehicles, and my colleagues' chatter, my mind kept on turning back to Auntie Rajni, and I wondered why. She stayed in a two-storey bungalow next door, one which had yellowed with age and yet was remarkably well kept. Auntie Rajni had entered this house as a young bride forty years ago. At that time, she had joined a unit comprising of a loving husband and doting in-laws. The years had been kind to them in all but one respect. They remained childless. However, her in-laws treated her like the daughter they never had and spoilt her rotten, much to the chagrin of the neighbourhood nosy parkers.

Life went on at a regular pace, replete with holiday jaunts, parties, friends, and acquaintances dropping in, mostly to partake of the wonderful food on offer in their house. Auntie Rajni, like her mother-in-law, was a wonderful cook, so their house was the repository of great joy, happiness, fun, and laughter.

Now, of course, what remained were just memories. As time passed, the family shrunk in size. First, her mother-in-law departed from this world. Her father-in-law, unable to bear the loss, passed away within a week. Her husband of thirty-five years, though healthy and robust, collapsed without any warning one day and died in his office. All of a sudden, Auntie Rajni was all alone and coping with her sorrows. But the loneliness was not for long because one day she was found walking in the park with a small pup.

That was how I met her at the park when I shifted next door a year ago because her dog took a fancy to me—or rather, my red trainers—as I jogged and dragged her by pulling at its leash towards me. She tried to check it, but it was a wasted effort, for the little thing just did not give up till it reached me. Once it did, it started wagging its tail playfully. She apologized for the intrusion and said that she was amazed at its behaviour because it had previously never showed any interest in a human being except for growling ferociously at them. This had been since the day he had, as a young pup, miraculously appeared from somewhere, slid under her iron gates, and propped himself on her veranda— for keeps!

And that was how, on the days that followed, we fell into a routine. I went for a jog around the park, and Auntie walked Baddie, the dog. Usually, we stopped to chat awhile before dispersing. Sometimes, Auntie invited me for dinner, while at other times, she came over to my place. Whenever I visited her, Baddie would be shut in another room because he never let us chat in peace.

Today, as we drove along, I recollected the meeting in the evening. I had met Auntie after fifteen days, for I had been getting back home very late from work. Over the last few months, I now realized that she had become a surrogate mother to me. My thoughts were interrupted as we reached our destination.

The party went on till the wee hours of the morning, and I returned home, hitting the sack immediately. I woke up really late, having missed my morning jog. After the regulation stretching after getting off the bed, I pottered to the kitchen to fix my morning cup of tea and put the pan on the gas stove. Having done that, I sauntered across to my front door to pick up the morning newspaper and froze in my tracks, for there was a police jeep in front of Auntie Rajni's house.

Without as much as a blink, I ran across, pushing my way through the stray curious onlookers staring into the house. A policewoman was gently talking to Auntie Rajni, who looked pale and weak and was sitting on her sofa. I went and sat next to her while policemen scoured around the house. As I held her hand, the story was slowly revealed.

At seven in the morning, a patrol vehicle had caught a drug addict running away from Auntie Rajni's house. He had apparently tried to break into the house to steal things and was running away when the beat constable caught him. While he shook him a little roughly, the thief yelped and said that he should treat him gently, for he had nearly died after being attacked by a dog in that house.

At that, I looked around for Baddie. Not seeing him, for he would be locked in the room with so many people in the house, I told Auntie that I was going up to his room to give him a hug. There was a momentary silence, and then Auntie said, 'Baddie's not there.'

'But where is he?' I asked her. Not wanting to trouble her, I went ahead and looked around the house for some time but could not find him.

Thoroughly confused, I went back to the living room. 'Auntie, where on earth is Baddie? I have searched the entire house, and he is nowhere in sight!'

There was not a sound from Auntie, who stared frozenly ahead. Laying a hand on my shoulder, the policewoman said, 'If you are talking of madam's dog, he died five days back.'

Auntie wept like a child in pain!

11

Hustle in a Bustle

As usual, the airport was a frenetic hub of activity. The taxi line was full, and double parking added to the mayhem, with many cars parked lopsidedly; there were harassed passengers having their trunks opened or their stooges (depending on the passengers' social standing) looking around for a trolley, the paid porter (a new entrant these days) sidling up in the hopes of a good earning with an additional tip, the traffic controller whistling frantically. Oh yes, it was chaotic!

Amidst all that clamour and din, I saw a really obese lady alight from a Mercedes. She was quite a sight, clad in an outfit into which she had been squeezed, a Hawaiian shirt replete with yellow sunflowers, baggy trousers, fluorescent flip-flops and, yes, a hat, one of those big shady ones with a huge brim. Talk about making a grand entrance! I could almost visualize a red carpet to welcome Her Highness.

It was impossible to miss her in spite of the fact that there was the hassle of catching a flight in an hour and a half and the long lines coupled with the sight of the millions standing at the entrance, which made my heart do a flip. They did say that the counter closed forty-five minutes prior to departure, but with these snaky queues and the security personnel peering first at the ticket and then at the identity card to closely scrutinising your face, it was a Herculean task to fathom when entry into the hallowed portals of the terminal would be made possible.

And then there was a minor fracas because a kid did not have an identity card. Oh my god, these guys were such morons! From where would a four-year-old conjure up an identity card? The airport manager was called, and the group moved to the side as the rest of us inched ahead. Tempers were hitting a new high; I hoped that there wouldn't be a riot out there when, after having been made to feel like the FBI's Most Wanted, I was allowed to walk in.

Into the parlour, said the spider to the fly.' I wondered why that line kept humming in my head.

Fortunately, I had prebooked my seat and just needed the boarding card. Since I was not carrying any check-in baggage, I went to one of those newfangled stand-alone kiosks which stood quite a distance away from the regular check-in counter. As I gingerly made my way to the sign which stated that people with hand baggage only could use the contraption, some of my inner confusion-cum-quandary must have shown on my face, for soon a polite and courteous young man wearing the ground staff uniform materialized from nowhere and guided me through the tricky process of extracting my boarding pass from the machine in a jiffy.

Fully armed and tagged, I clomped towards security. There too was a mini Kumbh Mela. It was worse than any railway station; the only thing missing was a tea vendor shouting, 'Chai garam!' But the line did move. Miss Hawaii, with her enormous bulk, was a little ahead of me. Presumably, her entry through another gate had been smoother than mine, for she had reached the security check area before me. However, in front of me was a particularly annoying family where the lady was loaded to the gills with mismatched jewellery, the harassed husband on a business call, and a particularly truant child who kept on running around in circles till I started feeling dizzy just looking at her.

The line moved and reached the X-ray machine. Madame Hawaii put her Louis Vuitton handbag and a small suitcase on to it. The attendant pushed all the oddments placed on the conveyor leading to the X-ray unit jerkily. Miss Hawaii got all fired up and started raining abuses on the handler. 'How dare you handle my stuff so roughly!' she screamed. The poor man, probably shell-shocked by her size, just mumbled something. She huffed and panted towards the security for checking while her belongings moved through the screening machine.

Oh whew. Finally I had my chance. It went off smoothly for me. When I got myself frisked, checked, and cleared, I went to collect my handbag, and there she was at it again, arguing loudly.

They had detained her bag and wanted to see the contents. She protested against what she called harassment and demanded to see the top man at security. The impassive man standing between her and the bag did not budge an inch and said that they needed to see the round object in her bag. She refused, and there was a tug of war, then the handle of the bag flew open and . . . out jumped a black cat!

The last I heard as I went towards boarding were shrieks and the person at the counter explaining airline policy to her.

12

Memories

Abha woke up completely drenched. Some nightmare it had been! With shaking hands, she held on to the side of the mattress for support, heaved herself off the bed, and made her way to the bathroom. Her clothes stuck to her body like a second skin. She opened the door, stumbled into the bathroom, located the switch, and looked at herself in the mirror above the washbasin. Opening the tap, she splashed cold water on to her face. Brrrr, it was freezing cold. But then smiling wryly, she thought, *what else could one expect in December?*

Wiping her face dry with a towel, she went back to her bed, rearranged the bedclothes, and switched on the percolator. The clock showed 4 a.m. Time for a cup of tea as sleep was nowhere in sight.

She opened the window and looked out. *Dawn is still a long way off,* she mused. She went back and poured out the tea into a cup, picked it up, and then sat down in the armchair by the window. And that was when reaction set in.

A few days back had been her daughter, Nisha's, fifth birthday party. The kiddies' party had finished at seven o'clock, but the adults (Alok's friends and her pals) had had dinner and just left, for it had also been their seventh wedding anniversary. It was a combo of a kiddies' party plus a late-evening party—enjoyable but very tiring indeed!

Alok's voice wafted over to the kitchen. 'Hey, Abha, drop everything you are doing and come here.'

She ran out, still bedecked in all her finery and skidded to a stop before him in the study. Alok was a handsome man, although not in a conventional sense, for he did look a bit scholarly! However, the smile on his face that he turned on her was one full of love and affection.

He stood up, came to her, and whispered into her ears, 'Sweetheart, you took the shine out of everybody else today.

You really are an angel, dear, and now here is my little gift to you.' Saying that, he pointed to a gift-wrapped brown package on the table. 'Open it,' he said.

With heightened anticipation, she opened it, and her eyes goggled in shock. 'Goodness, w-where did . . . did you get this from?' she stuttered.

He just smiled gently and ruffled her hair. It was a special edition of *Complete Works of Shakespeare* (an edition sixty years old)!

She was dumbstruck for a moment, and then she turned to give him a tight hug. 'Just what I wanted, darling! You must have spent a lot of money to get this.'

'Shh! Shh!' said Alok. 'For you, my precious darling, I can willingly pay any price. You just keep smiling the same smile that smote a million hearts and bowled me over at the first instance!'

Wonderingly, she caressed the leather-bound cover. Ah, the smell of old paper; there was nothing on earth to beat that! She had at that moment decided that she would begin reading it the next day, beginning with *Macbeth*! As if it were a delicate object, she picked it up and went to her room, where she placed it on her bedside table. Having done that, she moved towards the doorway, planning to close down the kitchen.

She could hear Alok pottering around in the study. Through the bay windows of the drawing room, she could hear the wind blowing. *Looks like rain,* she thought to herself. Clearing away the junk accumulated from the party, she switched off the kitchen lights and proceeded towards the drawing room windows. There was a flash of lightning, followed by a sudden crackle of thunder, and then, all of a sudden, the lights went out!

Hell, she thought, *hope Nisha doesn't wake up and get scared.*

'Alok,' she called, 'just go and check on Nisha, please!' There was no answer. *He must be in the bathroom,* she thought. *Okay! Let me go to her!*

As she veered around in the darkness towards her daughter's room, she stumbled into something. 'Eeks!' she shrieked and then calmed down as strong arms held her. Oh, Alok! 'Alok, where were—'

Suddenly, one the arms holding her tightened, and the other clamped over her mouth. She froze, her scream broken midway. This was not Alok. Tears coursed down her cheeks! There were three of them. Uncouth, loutish, smelly men ransacked the entire house! They ate all the leftovers and drank up the liquor in the bar, but they did not stop there. They also proceeded to tie up Alok in a chair, and when he protested and threatened them with the police, they picked up a rod and hit him on the head. He was bleeding profusely, all tied up; they left him to die and also tied and gagged her up. After this, grinning evilly, they picked up her little one and took her away.

All night, with the elements at their worst, tied to a staircase railing, she watched over her dead husband. The morning brought in the milkman and, finally, help was at hand. Alok was taken away on a stretcher in an ambulance, but it was too late—she knew he was no more. Her neighbours gave her solace, but her world had collapsed!

*   *   *

Nisha, now a beautiful twenty-year-old, had her mother's beautiful, delicate looks. She glanced at the once-handsome man by her side and then back to where his gaze lay. Ahead, in a corner of the room overlooking a garden, sat a woman lost in her own world.

'Papa!' said Nisha. 'I am getting married tomorrow, and you will be all alone! How on earth will you manage all by yourself? It's going to be lonesome.'

Sadly, Alok turned towards his only child and, gently cupping her face in her hands, said, 'Darling, I shall not be alone. Your mum will always be with me! I can't forget what the criminals did to her that night. She lost her mind after they tortured and raped her before me! Don't know what she thinks or whether she is capable of thought, but I have both of you, and I could have lost both of you. The police were quick in saving you, but I couldn't save her. She is mine,' he said, tears pouring down his cheeks, 'and I cannot leave her.'

Rocking in her armchair, Abha smiled wistfully as she watched a butterfly emerging from its chrysalis!

13

The Dark Knight

I was driving back home after a particularly late night party along with two totally sozzled colleagues, and it was my duty to deposit them safely at their houses in one piece. One of them started singing sad songs, those sung in the days of yore by the great old-timer Mukesh, while the other wept copiously in accompaniment. I rolled my eyes upward, 'Thank God, they haven't thrown up in my car!' I thought, then amended hastily, 'Yet!'

I am a thorough teetotaler. Do not get me wrong, for I am not against drinks; it's just that the 'nectar of the gods' and yours truly do not click. Somehow, I have never acquired the taste for it.

Traffic at that time was thankfully meagre. I guess, with the next day being a working day and with these narrow feeder roads traversing through residential areas, even the huge trucks trundling down the highway had no business venturing in. Bundle 1 was deposited into the arms of the security guard at the apartment block where he resided. I waited long enough to see him led into the lift and then shifted gears and drove on for the next couple of kilometres to offload my next co-passenger. His wailing had subsided to a series of sobs interspersed with hiccups. As I neared his gate, I saw him sit ramrod straight in his seat. All of a sudden, his sobs subsided, and something akin to panic began to appear in his eyes.

Figures, I thought caustically. His nemesis, in the form of his dad, a retired brigadier, a highly decorated stalwart of the Indian Army, was enough to make him sober up. As I braked to a stop and leaned across to open his door, he stiffly stepped out to charted territory, probably quaking in his knees and trying hard not to show it. *Welcome to the dragon's lair,* I thought. I honked as I left, noting with satisfaction that the interior lights in the bungalow had come on. And they would not be switched off in a hurry, as I would be informed by the army progeny the next day.

Whew, now for home sweet home. As I drove on through the deserted streets with just the street lights on, I longingly thought of the comfort of my bed. It had been a long day in the office and then followed the birthday party of our senior colleague. As I drove on, I saw the lights of an ATM ahead and slowed down to a standstill. I remembered that some money had to be withdrawn to pay the electrician in order to buy and install a geyser. It was getting chilly already. Winter appeared to be setting in fast. I stopped before the ATM, and my eyes automatically veered towards the scene in front of me.

A young woman was just coming down the stairs leading to the ATM. A couple of guys who had just alighted from the car in front of me were moving towards the ATM. They, on a closer examination, looked like boys who had had a drop too many. One was a burly six-footer, and the other was a good foot shorter but stockily built. As the duo climbed up the stairs, their gaze zeroed in on the woman coming down the steps. Like predators, they approached her and said something to her. The woman protested, but the taller one grabbed her and started dragging her towards their car.

As I charged out to help the lady in distress, I was startled by a flying object. Five-footer landed in a heap in front of me and was soon followed by six-footer. I stood agape as the lady, without as much as a glance at me, suddenly disappeared into the night. It was as if the men had just been punched and thrown by a giant fist. Strangely, there was not even a scratch or wound on them.

I looked at the two unconscious louts at my feet and, gathering my wits, dialled the number 100. Within minutes, the cops arrived and, after having a look at the two men on the ground, commended me in overpowering them. Apparently, the two were on the most wanted ATM robbers list. I quickly disabused them of my so-called heroics. I told them about the young lady who had, in the dim light, appeared to be in her twenties and who, having dealt with the errant creatures, had just vanished into the darkness of the night.

The cops looked at me quizzically. One of them patted me on the shoulder and said, 'You are lucky, young man, to be alive. These two shoot to kill, and only last fortnight, they had hit an ATM on the opposite side of the road and escaped. The camera in the booth had captured their images. A brave young woman who had resisted the robbery had been shot in the stomach and died on the way to the hospital. But, sir, now you have to come to the police station. We need you to complete a few formalities.'

They walked on to their PCR van with the culprits already handcuffed inside it. I turned towards my car with one of the cops accompanying me towards it in order to give me directions to the police station. He was scrolling through his mobile phone and looking at some images. He stopped at one, enlarged it, and showed me the picture of a girl. It was the brave heart who had died at the hands of the two animals.

Seeing it, I froze, for today's heroine and the girl in the picture were the same. The car keys fell out of my nerveless hand. As I bent down to pick them up, I saw a stream of blood trailing down the stairs.

14

Spanner in the Works

The grey facade of the newspaper office was, well, just that—grey! Standing in that solitary aloofness, having withstood the ravages of nature over the past hundred years, it looked quite depressing, especially on that cloudy evening; the exterior of the building competed with the greyness of the sky above.

The only welcoming aspect of it was the blaze of light which could be seen lighting up its interiors, looming large through the numerous windows peeping out to the world. But for Rakesh, with his massive brows carved into a frown, the darkness around him and the brightness within mattered not a whit, for he was furious.

Ever since the new Mister Know-It-All editor had taken over eight months back, the staff at the *Evening Chronicle* had not had a moment's respite. Work, of course, and extra work too was something everybody was used to, considering the fact that it was short-staffed and deadlines had to be met. But yesterday, his trip to the accounts department had left him seething. The medical bills of his sister, which had been astronomical, had not been cleared for over four months. The earlier editor had passed orders that all reimbursements should be made within a month without fail. Now, the silly clerk had the gall to tell him that the new editor had given instructions to keep all bills pending till he gave the go-ahead.

He had been left with no alternative but to seek a personal appointment with the editor today. Going up the stairs, he walked around the maze of corridors, passing various workstations, the noisy hubs of activity, to the last room at one end of the building. Entering the secretary's chamber, he reminded her that he had to meet the big boss. Neena, the secretary—usually a sweet, smiling young lady—was today looking distinctively sour. He asked her if she was okay, and she responded by saying that she was quitting in a week's time as working for the 'great man' was painful for 'lesser mortals' like her. On this cryptic note, she gestured towards him to enter the dragon's lair.

As he walked in, he remembered this room where, previously, one could walk in without knocking to the smell of cheroots wafting around and the warmth of the person manning the editorial desk. The then editor, for all his geniality, had been no pushover. A stickler for targets, he was willing to indulge in brainstorming in a tricky situation, fighting for his staff against the management, if required, and yet reigning with a firm hand. Yes, he had been a paragon of excellence while the one in position now was the complete antithesis of his predecessor.

Anyway, even if the prospect of meeting him was unpleasant, he had to thrash out his own matter. Knocking on the door, he was bid by a voice from within to enter. Pushing the door open, he walked up to the desk and looked into the cold eyes of the man before him.

Before he could open his mouth, Ajay said, 'Well, Rakesh, I have been looking at your work lately, and I find that the clues that you have been creating for your crossword puzzle are not up to the mark. You should aim for the standard of *The Guardian*.' He smirked.

Rakesh was too stunned at first to react. Gathering his wits, he said, 'Sir, our readers seem to be happy with it. In fact, our reviews indicate that our circulation has increased due to the new format, where the jumbled anagrams of the clues at, say, "four down" through a particular week are finally formulated into words which, when placed in a particular order, indicate a proverb, a book's title, or even a line of some well-known poem. For instance, this week, the clues and the words generated by it would form the title *Far from the Madding Crowd*. We do mention how many words would be used and the nature of the puzzle—a book, a line from a song, or whatever be the subject picked up.'

Very casually, Ajay flicked the contents of his mouth into a spittoon that he held with his hand, a hand encircled with garish red beads, and said that Rakesh had to pull up his socks for he wanted things to function in his way. The 'or else' was left hanging in mid-air.

Rakesh swallowed his rising ire and, in a subdued manner, said, 'Sir, my sister's medical bills have not been cleared by the accounts department. It's been months since they were submitted.'

Mr Editor looked up and said, 'Sonny, I want results, not whiners.'

At that, Rakesh erupted, 'Sir, that is my money that you are holding on to. You have no right to do that.'

With an icy look, Ajay said, 'Come and see me after two weeks. I am too busy today. We can discuss this again.'

Rakesh looked at him silently for a minute. Both glared at each other, and finally, he turned and walked out. Neena looked at him sympathetically, shrugged her shoulders, and raised her eyes heavenward with a look replete with sympathy.

Rakesh went back to his desk and wrote out his resignation. Of course, the mandatory notice period would have to be worked out. His closest friend, Anil, who was in charge of the fashion page for the newspaper, looked at him and asked him in concern, 'Rakesh, are you going to burn down the building? You look as if you are going to destroy it.' Not getting a reply, he continued, 'Brother, what is the matter?'

It was as if a dam broke. Rakesh narrated the encounter with the boss and said, 'Anil, will you please go through my stuff as you usually do, but with extra care because, in my

state of mind, I am bound to make mistakes.' Anil readily
agreed and said he would help him out.

From that day onwards, Rakesh worked like a zombie.
Staring into space and getting increasingly withdrawn,
he would jump at the slightest sound. Observing him, a
worried Anil suggested visiting a doctor. Rakesh refused;
he seemed maniacally possessed.

On a Saturday night after the day's work was over, as
was the routine, Anil borrowed from Rakesh the set of
crossword clues for the week. Reaching home and after a
quick dinner, he sat down to solve it by himself. By 2 a.m.
he had completed six of the clues, but the seventh, which
was supposedly the trick clue leading to the answer to that
week's solution indicating a murder mystery title completely,
foxed him! Finally, he gave up, deferring it for the morning
when the mind was fresh.

He woke up at 5 a.m., went through his morning rituals,
including a jog, and found that he was running late for his
morning shift. Oh well, he would complete the seventh
crossword on the way to work and surprise Rakesh, who
would be waiting for him after having completed his night
shift.

However, despite racking his brains, the answer
continued to elude him even on his bus ride to the office.
As he got down from the bus and walked to the office,
the answer flashed in his mind with a sudden ping: *By the
Pricking of My Thumbs*. Yes, that was the correct answer!
He literally ran towards the building with the knowledge
of having cracked it. As he began to approach it, he saw a
manacled Rakesh being brought down the steps. He lurched
forward and then stopped; Rakesh passed him while being

led towards the police jeep, muttering, 'By the pricking of my thumbs.'

On a stretcher, a covered body was being carried to the waiting ambulance; its limp, lifeless hand had red beads around the wrist.

15

The Message Trail

Neha thought happily that she was the luckiest girl in the world. She smiled at her mother, who had just come in to check on her. Her mother, Smriti, looked at Neha with doting eyes. For it was Neha's wedding day, and what a beautiful bride she made. She was a blessing from the Almighty, for she had been born after fifteen years of marriage. After numerous trips to various holy destinations, to doctors, and even to astrologers, they had given up hope when suddenly happiness entered their lives. Neha brought in sunshine and laughter into the lives of her husband, Sudhir, and her.

Suddenly shaking off her sentimental reminiscences, she went over to her daughter, who was surrounded by her friends, and fussed over the folds of her outfit.

'Oh, Ma!' said Neha. 'Stop being such a busybody. Just sit down and relax.'

Smriti looked at her and said, 'Easy for you to say. Wait till your own daughter gets married.'

Before Neha could say something, her attention was drawn to her phone beeping a message. Her face froze the moment she looked at it. As always, it was a message for her. She composed her face and asked her mother if she could have a soft drink as her throat was parched. Smriti glanced at her fondly, having missed the momentary panic-ridden expression on her daughter's face, and nodded her head as she went away.

With trembling hands scrolling through her phone to open the message, Nisha looked at it. It said: 'Darling, the pink colour suits you very well, but you should have taken an orange tone with a golden hue. You would have looked like a golden bride.' As usual, it was a new number, and as she had done earlier in the past six months, she deleted this particular message too and blocked the number.

It had all started on one of the days at work. As a fresher on the job, she had a lot of interaction with clients. Some customers were pushy; some even made passes. Well, there were people of varying temperaments, and she knew how to handle them. Being beautiful, of course, was a handicap at times, but she was down to earth and never stooped to calculate her worth in terms of her beauty. Her parents had inculcated in her all the qualities which went into the creation of a good human being.

Suddenly, out of the blue, one day she got a message on her mobile. It said: 'Sweetheart, come for a cup of coffee. You look really ravishing in white.' The number was unknown. She tried dialling it, but the identification software in her phone drew a blank, and the voice message stated that the number did not exist. For the next few days, the same trend followed. Every day she received a message, each pointing out things which only her family and she would be aware of.

One message asked her if she had enjoyed the Spider-Man movie with her friends. The other admonished her for laughing and joking with her male colleagues at the coffee-and-burger diner where there had been a birthday treat celebration. After five such messages, she blocked the number. Then there was a lull for a few days. Just when she had begun to relax, another message from yet another number complimented her on her new hairstyle. That was blocked too, but it was soon followed by another, which said that her car had low pressure in the rear left tyre. It was true.

That was when she told her mother. A complaint was filed at the local police station, but though the policemen were sympathetic, they could not achieve a breakthrough. It was as if a SIM card was sent for a single or a few messages and then destroyed.

Summer gave way to the monsoon. The messages stopped coming. One day, when she walked into her house, her parents were seen to be in conversation with a personable young man. He stood up when she entered. Her mother introduced him to her, saying, 'This is Avinash. Remember,

Dad used to talk about Uncle Ravi and his wife, Rama, in the US? They were our neighbours and good friends fifteen years ago at Chandigarh before they moved out to the States. This is their son. He had come looking for us. He is a partner in a law firm in Mumbai.'

In an undertone, her mother whispered that his parents were no more after a freak accident on the expressway in the US cut short their lives two years back. Turning to Avinash, she told him that she would get him a cup of coffee and that he should feel at home. Saying that, she bustled into the kitchen.

Avinash smiled at her, and they started chatting. It was an enjoyable evening, with him accepting her parents' invitation to join them for dinner. Slowly, they became friends and started meeting regularly. Then one Sunday, during a drive to the suburbs, he proposed to her, and she accepted with alacrity, trying to control the waves of happiness flooding her mien.

Since then, life had been moving at the pace of a whirlwind, but now, this disturbing occurrence again. *Okay,* she thought, *I shall be moving from here. Maybe this will stop now.*

The marriage was solemnized amidst great festivities, and the young couple went for a honeymoon and soon settled into domestic harmony. She also got transferred to Mumbai. Life was blissful when, suddenly after two months, it started again.

The first one was innocuous; it said: 'You should drive slowly in the rain.'

And then they started coming in with alarming regularity.

'You should not have left Pune. I miss you.'

'You were throwing up at lunchtime. Are you pregnant?'

She showed them to her husband, who was really furious and said that he was going to the police. She stopped him, saying that it was of no use and repeated the episodes at Pune to him. He said that it would not do to sit quietly while the stalker intruded into their lives. Moreover, it was having an adverse impact on her. Coming to a decision, he said that he would take her to Delhi and, from there, on to Shimla, where she could take a break.

She looked bewildered at the sudden plans and said, 'Now?'

'Yes,' he said, 'even the stalker will not know of our plans if we leave immediately.' He also cautioned her from informing her parents and the office, saying that maybe their phones had been hacked or tapped. She could inform them from Shimla itself. So they took the next flight out to Delhi and drove down to Shimla.

It was a blissful holiday. She thought that she was blessed in having such a caring husband. And then on the last day of the vacation, her phone pinged again.

'Today is the last day of your vacation and also of your life!'

The phone slipped out of her nerveless fingers.

'What happened?' asked Avinash.

'Nothing,' she said and smiled and picked up her purse. 'Shall we go?' she asked.

As she went to open the door, suddenly she was jerked back. And as she felt fingers closing in round her throat in a vice-like grip, the door crashed open, and she suddenly fell to the ground, gasping for breath.

Her mother rushed to her with tears streaming down her cheeks. 'Sorry, beta, I led you into this. But thank God you had told me of your plans before he stopped you from passing on information of your unscheduled trip.'

Bewildered, she looked at her and the police posse which had taken her husband to custody.

'You are lucky, madam,' the inspector said. 'This man is a murderer of wives. You would have been the thirteenth! We had zeroed in on him due to the tracking of his mobile handset. The messages in Mumbai emanated from one location—your home—while you were at the office. And, madam, how much insurance cover had you taken, fifteen lakhs? The nominee was your husband, of course.'

Avinash looked daggers at her as he was led away.

16

The Route

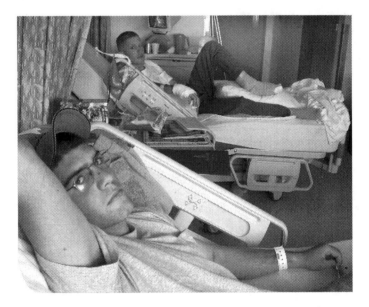

It was a lovely winter morning. Abhishek, as was his
wont, was enjoying the drive. Thankfully, unlike the
previous day, it was not foggy at all. It was bright and sunny.
The canopy of trees lining the winding road looked like a
welcoming bower. This was a route normally not taken by
motorists, for it was skirting the border of the town with

not much habitation around. Most people felt comfortable travelling bumper to bumper on clogged roads.

Comfort in numbers, he thought wryly. Anyway, the lack of traffic suited him. So he was able to relax and drink in the surroundings as he drove.

As he turned round the bend, out of the blue, suddenly a jogger appeared on the wrong side of the road. He slammed the brakes with full force, twisting the steering wheel completely in the opposite direction. *Screech!* And the car ground to a halt a few yards away.

Rushing out, he ran to the prone figure on the ground. It was a relief to find that the man was still breathing. There was a gash where the driver's side mirror had hit him while brushing past him and the gash on his head was probably made while hitting the stone rubble lying around on the ground. Bundling him into the car, he drove at breakneck speed to the nearest hospital. On reaching there, he drove up to the emergency admissions area, got off, and beckoned to the waiting attendants, who came running instantly. Immediately, a stretcher was organized, and the injured person was gently taken out of the car and into the hospital.

Abhishek followed them in and completed the routine formalities for admission. A resident doctor asked for details of the patient. Abhishek explained the situation to him, saying he had found him on the road, and handed over the injured person's identity card. He had taken it out from the wallet which had fallen out of the person's pocket as he had collapsed. He did not mention that the gentleman he had brought in had been hit by his car. It would have unnecessarily complicated matters.

Thankfully, the car had not suffered any damage to indicate that it was the vehicle which had caused the accident. The patient wouldn't have had time to recognize the car too because he had come up on it round the bend and the events had occurred within a span of seconds—too short a period to register any details. The hospital guys would probably have called the cops, and that was an irritant that he could do without. The doctor nodded and asked him to wait while they attended to the patient. He assured him that the injuries did not appear to be serious. 'Just a matter of regaining consciousness,' he added with a reassuring smile.

Abhishek decided to have a cup of tea in the cafeteria of the hospital while he waited. After half an hour, he got a call on his mobile. It was the doctor. He said that the patient had recovered and that he wanted to meet his saviour. Having paid his bill, he proceeded towards the reception, where he was directed towards the inpatient department.

He entered the private room, cap in hand, to where his boss, the cantankerous millionaire, Rajan Agarwal, awaited him. With a grateful smile, the industrialist turned towards him as he opened the door and walked in.

Serves the sucker right! He shouldn't have shouted at me yesterday, Abhishek thought as he walked in an obsequious manner towards the bed.

17

Déjà Vu

Sujata was peeved and with good reason too. For after a particularly tedious day at work, she had walked home to the thought that she would have a nice steaming cup of coffee, settle down into her favourite armchair, relax and feel better. But the trip to the fridge revealed that she had run out of milk, and the wretched cook had failed to inform her of this fact. There was no point in yelling at him for this lapse for the unrepentant creature would just put on a woebegone expression on his face and simply say that he had forgotten. These hired help were more of a liability than an asset. The word *help* was a misnomer.

So there she was on the way to a convenience store, all set to stock up on her milk supplies. *The trials and tribulations one faces daily,* she thought wryly.

All of a sudden, she saw a lady walking towards her widen her eyes in horror, gesticulating and pointing towards something behind her. She turned and a wordless shriek passed her lips, for there was an SUV swerving dangerously towards her. She jumped aside in the nick of time as the vehicle hit the kerb and ground to a halt.

Shaken but furious, she bounded towards the car and found two occupants, a boy and a girl, both in their early twenties. The young boy had the slightly unfocused look of one who had imbibed a glass too many. She went up to him and said, 'Come along, we are going to the police station.'

Hearing that, the other occupant in the vehicle, a petrified girl, got out and came to her side. Taking her hands in her own, she said, 'Ma'am, please let us go. My parents don't know that I am out with him. If you complain, they will be called. Just this time, please let us go. I promise it won't happen again.'

The girl's woebegone face reminded her of her own wild youth, and taking pity on her, she said, 'All right, but mind you, you have got away lightly. This could have been a very serious incident.' Retracing her steps, the girl nodded mutely while her eyes showed her gratefulness. The car revved up and was soon gone. Shaking her head, Sujata completed her chores and went home.

* * *

Autumn was in the air, the best season according to her. She was back to her favourite city after a break of five years. Nothing had really changed except for the fact that the population had spiralled. *Being a senior executive has its advantages,* she mused. Creature comforts were aplenty. However, having worked continuously at a stretch till late in the evening, she decided to give her driver a break in order to exercise her stiff body. She started walking towards her house, which was just three kilometres away.

The night air was pleasant. People milled around the streets. Cars zoomed past. Strangely, the traffic was not very heavy. In any case, she welcomed the paucity of vehicles on the road. She moved on steadily and briskly, when all of a sudden, she saw the person walking towards her start gaping in shock.

As if in slow motion, she turned to see a huge dark vehicle hit a pedestrian with the simultaneous squealing of brakes. She rushed towards the injured person and, at the same time, called for an ambulance from her phone. Gently turning the prone body, she cradled the head on to her lap and saw the face through the rivulets of blood flowing through a gash. Suddenly, the glimmer of recognition dawned. It was the girl in the car that had nearly hit her a few years back. Slowly, she stirred and, trying to raise her head, was feebly muttering a few words.

Someone amidst the crowd of bystanders had called the police. The errant driver had been rounded up and was standing right in front.

Oh my god, it's this girl's boyfriend! she realized in shock. But no, this time, there was another girl with him.

The victim whispered, 'I tried . . .' And then she was suddenly still.

18

The Nest

It had been a particularly turbulent flight until then, and she had not got her morning cuppa coffee because the stewardess had politely and with the oh-so-fixed smile on her visage informed her, 'Ma'am, I am so sorry, but due to turbulent weather, we cannot serve you hot beverages.'

Lack of coffee did to her what absence of heroin did to a smack addict. So she spent the remainder of the time in the flight shooting daggers at the 'lady in the sky' even though she knew that the latter was following due procedure.

She herself would have made a lousy stewardess. How could one perfect the art of maintaining a vacuous, vacant smile, particularly when one heard the continuous bleat (oops, sorry that wasn't very diplomatic of her) of the passengers, most of whom had a fetish for constantly summoning the 'hired help'. For this was the way most of her fellow travellers in her country viewed air hostesses. They were there to serve them tea, coffee, water, *biskoots*, and *kaju*; the last two items being biscuits and cashewnuts for the benefit of the international traveller. They, in fact, saw nothing wrong in their loutish behaviour. Thank God, ambrosial fluids were banned on domestic flights!

Anyway, the flight ended up doing what all flights did—land at its destination. But getting off was easier said than done, for this bunch of passengers was a particularly uncivilized one. Everyone seemed to be in a tearing hurry.

It is, she thought sourly, *as if they would be locked up in the aircraft if they did not get off the plane in twenty seconds.*

She prepared to wait patiently for the initial rush to die down. But that was not to be, for right in front of her, she saw a young man, probably in his early twenties, jostling a frail old lady who was standing timidly and trying to retrieve her cabin baggage.

That was the last straw!

'Excuse me,' she said, her voice clearly carrying, and the frenetic activity suddenly stopped as if frozen in time.

People turned towards her—some curiously, others dismissively—but no, not the errant traveller. It had not made an iota of difference to his insufferable actions.

'Hey you, the fellow in the red checked shirt!' she yelled, for by now, she was furious. 'Is your mother dying?' she shouted.

The man turned aggressively and bore down on her. 'What do you mean?' he growled.

She repeated, 'Is your mother dying, or did she abandon you at birth?'

'Listen, lady,' he began before she cut him short. Raising the old lady's arm, she pointed towards the long scratch mark caused by the buckle on the man's knapsack as he had brushed past her. She continued her tirade, 'I thought that maybe, since you were in such a hurry and pushed her so roughly, it was presumably due to a family emergency.'

Another middle-aged man piped in knowingly, 'This generation has no respect for elders.'

The young man reddened and apologized to the lady who by now had shrunk perceptibly, probably overawed by all the attention focused on her. All of a sudden, peace and calm descended in the environs of the aircraft, and people started disembarking quietly and systematically. The air hostess, the one who had refused her coffee, literally beamed at her as she got off.

Thankfully, she did not need to wait for her luggage because she was travelling without any. In any case, she was going home. Although, it had been five years since had been home, Mum would certainly have left her cupboard untouched. So all her clothes and bric-a-brac would be there for her use, for she still remained the same in terms of dimensions, height, weight, and volume. Dad had said that she would need to walk to the car park where he would be waiting.

Dear Dad! She thought smilingly. Nothing had really changed. Mum would have her favourite *aloo ka paratha* ready, waiting to be devoured. A cake would have been baked, cut, sliced, and ferreted away out of sight from prying eyes, especially Dad's.

As she walked out of the airport, trying to call Dad on his mobile, it was as if she had returned home from university for a vacation. Her five years of absence—which encompassed an elopement, being totally cut off from her parents, and then a tumultuous divorce—was as if it had never happened.

Drat the network! The disembodied voice intoned, 'This telephone number does not exist.' Just when she was about to redial, instinctively her eyes scanned the car park, and it was then that she spotted him and ran. Dear Dad! He was leaning against the bonnet of his car, the one he let no one touch, let alone drive.

As she reached him, time stopped, and she was his little one again. Hugging him, she was surprised to see a hint of moisture in his eyes. *No.* She shook her head. *Not Dad!* She must be mistaken. He had never showed any signs of weakness ever! In fact, all her reserves of strength were derived from the way he had lived life and conducted himself in all the years that she had seen him while growing up.

As her handbag was dumped on the back seat, she talked nineteen to the dozen exclaiming at the changes in the city, not noticing that her father was unusually silent. It was a short drive. Within ten minutes, they reached home. Unlocking the car door, she rushed to the gate, opened it, and gaily yelled, 'Mummy!'

As she walked in, the door was opened by the servant. She shouted, 'Mummy, where are you?' Not finding her in the kitchen, she rushed upstairs. Walking into her parents' bedroom, she stopped short. Her mother was sitting in a wheelchair, looking back at her without a trace of recognition in her eyes.

Her father hugged her wordlessly as tears streamed down his face and whispered, 'Alzheimer's.'

19

On the Mountain Track

Summer, especially coming on the heels of a particularly hard spell of winter, was always warmly welcomed by the residents of the hills not just for climatic reasons but also for the commercial angle, for it brought with its advent tourists who kept pouring in and boosted the economy.

However, he did not appreciate the flood of people climbing up from the plains, most of whom were noisy and irksome. They constantly rubbed him the wrong way, and that usually led to him getting worked up into a frenzy. Lately, the newfangled travel agents had taken to bringing in more and more people ostensibly on treks. The outsiders trampled on the wildflowers fringing the countryside and littered the area without any compunction.

Every day, there would be a noisy group coming up to his gate to gawk at the architectural marvel that was his home. Built during the times of British rule, the design of the grey sandstone mansion followed the Victorian model containing scalloping, lancet windows, and columned arches. It constituted a flagrant intrusion into his privacy.

His faithful old retainer, Rana, ambled up to him with his daily concoction of ginger-infused tea and, after setting it down on the table next to him, turned towards the dog, Rover. But before he could call him for his breakfast, as he did every day, something stopped him in his tracks. The master was watching the old video again.

Oh, well, it's one of those days again, he thought resignedly. The master would now slowly get into one of those moods, and all the staff, excluding him, would try to become invisible. He was the only one who could and did bear the brunt of the master's volatile behaviour. But then, he also knew how to deal with it, for he had been with the family from the time of the master's parents. In fact, he was the one who helped him in getting out of these moods.

Getting back to the aforementioned video, which was the catalyst for the fluctuating atmosphere in the house, it was the recording of the marriage ceremony of the master years ago with the most popular girl in the area. The mansion had been totally overhauled and renovated by the master before the advent of the bride. The wedding had been spectacular, and the new bride had hardly taken any time in settling in. She had been very popular with the staff. Life had been beautiful and full of life then, for the lady of the house brought along with her a bubbling vivaciousness into the hitherto all-male household.

Until that fateful day! She had been standing in the garden, which was her favourite haunt. That was where she spent hours tending to and caring for her favourite plants. It had been raining heavily all day, replete with thunder and lightning. The master had been calling out to her to come back into the house, but she had refused laughingly and asked him to come out instead. Her trill of laughter could be heard over the sound of rain when, all of a sudden, there was a loud rumbling sound. Before anyone could react, a huge boulder atop the elevated slope behind her got dislodged, came hurtling down, and hit her on the head. She died without regaining consciousness on the fifth day in the hospital, leaving behind a shattered husband and a dog who kept on howling for days after the mishap.

Today, a busload of tourists had come to gape at the property from outside. There was a lot of noise, and when Rana hobbled over to the window to close it, the master stopped him, got up instead, and went and stood next to it.

All of a sudden, the sky darkened with streaks of lightning, and the rumble of thunder made their presence felt. In a flash, the master sprinted outside and, in the nick of time, pulled a woman away from the debris hurtling down the slope. Time stood still. Rover went and licked the shaken woman's face.

Sheltering from the elements, and taking permission from the owner, the guide took the group into the house, and it was then that she, the girl who had a lucky escape, saw it in front of her—the portrait. It was a giant painting of the lady of the house, who was a mirror image of her, sitting with a dog identical to the one at her heels.

Rana and the master smiled at each other and embarked on their much delayed journey with Rover.

20

The Open Closet

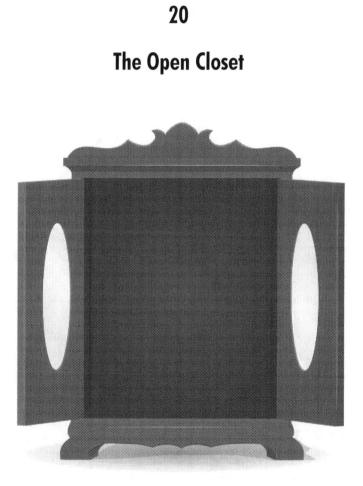

Ranbir looked up from his newspaper when Asha came to give him his morning cup of tea. She avoided his eyes as she put the cup down and turned to go away. Ranbir smiled wryly. Apparently, she had not forgiven him for yesterday. *A minor issue,* he thought, *had unnecessarily snowballed into a raging argument.*

She had asked him to accompany her on a shopping expedition to buy gifts for her numerous relatives. She was going to her parents' home for a couple of weeks. He had cried off from the trip, saying that he had some work to finish in office although it was a holiday. Just then, as he was getting ready to leave, his friend Vikas had landed up and dragged him away for a round of golf. When he got back home, the volcano had burst. Since then, he had been given the silent treatment.

'Asha,' he said in a gentle tone, 'let's go shopping.'

Instantly, her sulky face was transformed into a picture wreathed with smiles—all sins, real or imagined, forgiven.

Oh, the trials and tribulations of being a husband, he thought.

The expedition, contrary to his entrenched belief, had not been a nightmare. Shopping with a woman was an eye-opener; the mind-boggling varieties on display ensured that making a decision was a challenge. A psychologist would have loved to delve into the mind of a woman at that stage.

After a perfect lunch at a popular food court, they returned home. Asha was now her usual jovial self as she pinned name tags on to each packet being gift-wrapped and ready to be gifted to friends and relatives on her trip home. She was leaving the next day.

*   *   *

It had been a week since she had been at her parent's place, and she was dying to get back home to her husband. This was the first time she had left him within a year of their marriage, and she was missing him terribly. *Poor soul, how on earth is he managing by himself?* she thought. Although he kept assuring her that he was managing beautifully and that she should enjoy herself, her thoughts kept on wandering back to her husband. Finally, she decided to cut short her visit and return home.

Ma had tears in her eyes at the departure lounge of the airport. 'Such a short visit,' she said.

'Ma, I will come soon with your *damaad*(son in law),' she said, hugging her before she turned and left for checking in.

The flight was uneventful. She felt like a girl going out on her first date. *Come off it,* she scolded herself, *that's your husband you are going to.* Who would have thought that it had been an arranged marriage? She was head over heels in love with him and was now behaving like a teenaged lover.

Taking a cab home was no problem. In twenty minutes, she was at her front door after having paid off the cabbie. She rang the bell. There was no answer. Okay, maybe he was sleeping or had just gone out. Obviously, he could not have been waiting for her. He did not know that she was coming. He would definitely be surprised to see her two days before her scheduled arrival.

Rummaging into her purse, she found her spare key and let herself into the house, which was absolutely silent and still. *So he is out,* she thought as she walked into their bedroom. She stopped short. It was definitely her room, yet not hers. There was lingerie of various multi-coloured hues, high-heeled slippers, and nail enamel strewn on the bed.

Reeling in shock, she sobbed silently, for it was obvious that he had had a woman in here. Tears flowed incessantly as she held on to the doorway for support. The bathroom door opened, and both the players—the person coming from within, her husband, and she—looked at each other, transfixed. Her husband, the very macho and handsome Ranbir, was wearing an evening gown, replete with make-up and jewellery.

He would have made a very attractive woman, she thought as she debated whether to laugh or cry—laugh in relief that there was no other woman or weep because now there were two women in the house.

21

Watch and Ward

This is happening way too frequently, thought Dinesh as he looked at the beads of sweat on his brow. Standing in front of the mirror at 3 a.m. on a cold, wintry night and knowing that sleep would now elude him, he was annoyed, to say the least.

And tomorrow was a working day. His mother had gone away for a month on an official trip, and he had decided to sleep in her room. The temptation was the huge bed, a comfortably firm mattress, and the giant television screen. This was the third consecutive night that he had woken up. Maybe some noise was the cause. He checked the windowpanes, but they were all secure. The entire neighbourhood was in deep slumber. Even the perennially howling dogs were conspicuous by their absence. The neighbourhood watch scheme was presumably in the sleep mode.

Since he was wide awake, he decided to watch television. Even after surfing through various channels, he did not find anything to engage his fancy. Getting up from the sofa, he strolled into the kitchen. Rummaging through the cupboards, he found a packet of instant noodles. Putting some water into the saucepan and waiting for it to boil, he poured himself a glass of Coke.

Then all of a sudden, in the stillness of the night, he heard the bell ring. The clock showed 3.30 a.m. *Who could it be?* he thought irritably. He went to the door and checked through the peephole. There was no one. Maybe it was at the neighbour's. The silence could have magnified the sound beyond proportion and carried it through to him.

The seventh night of his mother's absence was a Saturday and a holiday too, and it was reason enough for a late night out with friends. He bade goodbye to his friend who dropped him home and, humming softly, went up to his door, treading the stairs softly so that the neighbours were not disturbed.

He unlocked the door and went in. The salubrious effects of liquor vanished in a jiffy. Something was quite not right, he felt. Without switching on the lights, his eyes tried to adjust to the darkness within. His sharp ears heard the sound of heavy breathing near the sofa. Quietly, he went towards the armrest on the farther side of the sofa and swooped down on to the dark shadow there and found something fleshy. Curving his hands around what was a muscular arm, he tried to pull it out. But although he was strong, the intruder, probably due to his desperation, managed to pull away after slashing at his arm with a knife.

Dinesh stumbled as he sought to regain his balance and, at the same time, try to ignore the shooting pain of the wound. While doing so, his fingers touched the switch of the lamp next to him.

All of a sudden, the room was flooded with light. The escaping intruder was caught unawares by the sudden brightness in the room. He staggered, and as his eyes fell on Dinesh, the expression on his face changed. The next moment, things took an unexpected turn.

The swarthy, muscular, and deadly creature in front of him was suddenly transformed into a blabbering mass of shaking jelly. Hysterically, he fell at Dinesh's feet and begged the Almighty for forgiveness.

The policeman taking him into custody said that he was a murderer on the loose. He had killed his brother in a property dispute. Thanking him as he led the prisoner away, the cop requested him to come to the police station the next day so that they could record his statement. Dinesh agreed to do so. As he retraced his steps back into the house, he wondered at the strange reaction of the intruder.

The next morning, he presented himself at the police station at the appointed time. The events leading to the arrest were minutely discussed. Finally, after an hour of questioning, the policeman thanked him and said that he could leave. While he was getting up, Dinesh mentioned that he did not know what had scared the prisoner so much at his home. He asked the officer if they had any clue about the bizarre behaviour of the person in custody.

Wordlessly, the inspector handed over a file to him. It was the case file of the culprit. Flipping through the pages, Dinesh's fingers froze on one page, the sheet containing a picture of the murdered brother. Dinesh was looking at his mirror image.

A doppelgänger, it was.

22

Prayers

Sammy was late again! Her ribboned plaits hanging loose, she bounded across the corridors, skipped down the stairs, and rushed to the playground in the fervent hope that he would not be there at least this once!

But as always, her prayers did not obviously reach their destination on time; very much like her, they took their own time in travelling more at the pace of a tortoise taking a breather. In any case, there he was right in front of her in the playground, glowering at her, arms akimbo on his hips. As she skidded to a stop in front of him, he asked her in grim tones, 'So what's the excuse for today's delay?'

She opened her mouth, beginning with her explanation to say that, as usual, it was sour-faced Sister Agnes again. The venerable lady had, with an uncanny precision of timing, thought of an errand for her to run. *Come to think of it,* she mused, *if she didn't know better, it appeared as if Sister was positively allergic to her, and she had a knack of knowing when she was trying to slip away from her waspish presence.* She had even insisted that she complete the task even after being informed that she had to leave for her practice.

Gathering her wits about her while stammering out her apology, she looked at him, but he had already turned away and was dribbling the ball and shouting instructions to the other girls. Forgetting Sister, she got into the spirit of the game, and even he, the handsome basketball coach, who was the heartthrob of the starry-eyed girls in her class, softened down enough to give her a pat on the back at the end of the session, though not before threatening to throw her off the team if she as much as landed up a few seconds late on the morrow.

Time, as was its wont, continued at its own pace. She continued with her passion for basketball and brought in major laurels for the school, then the university, and finally, for the state. Her ultimate achievement was when she made it to the national team too. She was not only a great player but also a very striking-looking one too.

The years passed by. Her classmates and friends went about their respective lines of study and careers. Contact was maintained, albeit at irregular intervals.

One day, out of the blue, she got a call from one of her oldest school friends, one she had been studying with since kindergarten. There was going to be a school reunion. Could she make it? She looked at her calendar, and by the sheerest coincidence, she was free on that day. The excitement at meeting her school pals was palpable.

The chilly winter morning did nothing to subdue the girls and their exuberance. After giggling through a lavish South Indian lunch, with the management keeping an anxious watch to check if their boisterousness got out of hand, they bundled into their hired cabs, which would take them to school.

The school loomed large in front of them—familiar yet not so familiar. The building was unchanged although the exterior paint had undergone a transformation from a sombre grey to a lively green. For a moment, time stood still, and there was silence all round—till the gatekeeper broke the spell by opening the latch with great gusto.

They trooped into the principal's office. The pretty PA there told them that she would escort them to the assembly room, where the Principal was waiting for them. They went as they had done years ago in pin-drop silence, for old habits died hard. Sammy looked ahead at the person being introduced to them as the principal, and it was no Mother Superior but a gentleman who was not a cleric.

Goodness! It was Mr Robinson, the basketball coach. The function passed off smoothly, with all the girls reminiscing about their time there before a crowd of rapt students.

After this was a round of introductions of teachers and staff. Out of the old-timers, just a couple remained. Sammy thought that one of them looked very familiar, especially with her stern demeanour. As they moved ahead, Mr Robinson, upon reaching the familiar face, said, 'You must remember her, your English teacher and now my wife, Mrs Robinson.'

Mrs Robinson looked at Sammy, and her smile froze. Sammy had her answer to her inexplicable skirmishes with the then Sister Agnes, now Mrs Robinson.

23

The Call

As a child, she had loved going to her grandparents' house, out of the confines of her closed 1,500-square-foot home and into the wide expanse of lawns, the backyard of the ancestral home, and the huge *aangan* (courtyard) replete with a raised platform housing the holy tulsi (basil)plant. Life had been wonderful then, pure fun and frolic, and the only burden casting a shadow were the inevitable school exams. But even they didn't really cause one to lose sleep or bring on nightmares.

She remembered the mango trees, the lone jackfruit tree, and the myriad of other trees like the gulmohar and the one bearing custard apples too. She loved spending the afternoon in the makeshift swing in the backyard. Her grandma, of course, used to admonish her if she as much as meandered towards her precious vegetable garden. Dadi, her grandmum, guarded her tomatoes, cauliflowers, or any seasonal vegetable sprouting out of the ground with the zeal of a soldier guarding the border.

What a wonderful period it has been, she thought as she drove up to the now-decaying mansion. The sound of silence and much more greeted her as she got off her vehicle and walked in through the gate to the front door. *For all its dilapidation,* she thought, *it is still in essence the same.* Now that she was back, she would do her best in restoring it.

She walked in through cobwebs and musty rooms, opening up the windows as she went. Climbing up the stairs and going into the first floor veranda, she paused to look down into the courtyard. The courtyard had been a hub of immense activity in those days. Jars of pickles would be kept out in the sun to cure them. Whole red chillies would be laid out to dry on plastic sheets prior to pounding them into powder. Young grandchildren would be paying hopscotch amidst squeals and claps of joy. Turning towards the outward longitudinal projection of three rooms, she found that the structure still looked a little incongruous given the stateliness of the main two-storey building.

The room at the far end was the kitchen complete with a wood stove, known colloquially as the *chulha.* Much to the chagrin of her *townie bahus*(daughters-in-law), Grandma used to insist on eating her meals cooked on that chulha only. None of the newfangled gas stoves for her, please, although there was one in the main building. What a tyrant she had been, and no one had the gumption to question her actions, including Grandpa, despite the fact that in his official capacity he was a cop and people trembled in his presence. At home, there was no doubt as to who was the cop!

Adjoining the kitchen was a storeroom, stocking all necessary items of daily use—cooking, cleaning, gardening, and other sundry stuff. The last room was connected to the main house and used to be permanently locked from outside. Only Grandma and her maid went in, for it housed an unspoken story. It contained an inhabitant, her aunt, who was physically there but mentally not just quite. In her younger days, she had seen her moving around the house. But the fact remained that she had seemed strange even then. She had told her one evening that she did not like girls, and since in that point in time she happened to be the only girl in the vicinity, it had to be her. But despite the malevolent glint in her eyes, she had not been scared of her. But sometimes, manic rage took over, and then she was like a veritable loose cannon. At such times, she would ferociously chase her younger sister and her cousin with a belt because the duo constantly messed around with her precious trunk, which was kept under lock and key and housed her worldly possessions. No one, however, knew what it contained.

With the passage of time, her moving around the house was restricted, and one fine day, without any announcement, she was relegated to that room. What an unfortunate soul. She had been married once, years ago, but had been sent back home by her husband within a week on the grounds that she was not quite right in the head.

Her eyes were drawn to the well in the courtyard, which she had studiously avoided even as a child. The well had a history. The said aunt had, in her teens, fallen into the well. Thankfully, the old retainer had seen her fall and had promptly raised the alarm. She had been drawn out of it in a bucket. Upon landing on terra firma, the first thing she said was that someone had pulled her in from inside. Apart from a gash on the head, outwardly, she seemed fine. But in the days that followed, she became prone to erratic behaviour. The worried parents got her married off, hoping that connubial bliss would stabilize her. But that was not to be.

Imperceptibly drawn towards the well, she went downstairs to it. Although it was partially covered by slats, she managed to peer into it—and drew back in terror. For through that stillness, she had clearly heard someone whisper her name from within.

The next day, labourers were called in to destroy the well. This work also entailed clearing out the debris inside it. After two days, one of the young hands came huffing and panting up to her and asked her to accompany him immediately. Wondering at his exhortations, she went out and stopped short. For amidst the heap was a skeleton with a ruby necklace round it, clutching at the frame of what had been a bucket.

There was no mistaking it. The necklace was a family heirloom. Her great-grandmother's portrait in the living room showed her wearing it. A case of a skeleton tumbling out from the closet or, as in this case, a well?

24

Stop

It was an exhilarating experience running downhill, skidding, slipping and simply not stopping—not because I would not but because I could not. After all, my body had not been designed with built-in brakes. So screaming and screeching with my hair all askew, I finally careered to a stop, nearly felling a young tree in the process. Well, I was quite agile for an almost thirty-year-old sedentary city damsel—almost! So I turned around with a triumphant look at my friends, who were still negotiating the slopes with varying degrees of terror, judging from the sound decibels emanating from them.

The rumbling brook with water gurgling across the boulders, and there were many of those—boulders, I mean—smooth, round, oval, ovoid specimens with nary a sharp edge, for years of aqueous pressure had smoothened the rough edges. At another level of bizarre thinking, I could examine an angular human being standing under a waterfall for aeons till he or she was transformed into a rounded personality. There went my overimaginative mind, going topsy-turvy into a spin, keeling over the edge as usual. Riotous images moved at kaleidoscopic speed, suddenly coming to a halt by something tugging at my jeans. Looking down, I stifled a smile, for it was a hungry mountain goat nibbling at my jeans and boots with a single-mindedness as if there was no tomorrow.

'Hang on, old fella! Wait, I have something for you.' Saying this, I took out a packet of biscuits and fed it to the clever rascal. Having chewed up an entire packet, the wily creature, without as much as a by your leave, vanished into a thicket. *So much for gratefulness,* I mused. I guess, mankind drew a lot into its make-up from such personalities in the animal kingdom.

I dropped my rucksack on to the ground and lay sprawled on the grassy slope near the pebbled brook. The shrieks of my friends, Aditi and Ramona, were becoming more discernable. I could spot Aditi's red jacket as she, sort of, roller-coastered down the slope. Ramona in her fuchsia-pink outfit daintily manoeuvred herself down the trail, aided by a walking stick.

Very prim and proper was Ramona, for she did everything by the book—planning the trek, bookings at the hotel, picking a guide. In a manner of speaking, it was good to have a planner; one did not have to bother about mundane things, like where to eat, sleep, etc. Aditi was the resident joker, with not a single serious bone in her body. She almost got kicked out of the office because she laughed while the boss berated someone for non-performance.

Later she told me, 'Rita, you do not know how hilarious it was at that moment. There was a yellow string on his bald pate, which moved snakily while he gesticulated.' That was Aditi for you. As for yours truly, I was the dreamer, head in the clouds, not caring to be bogged down by the humdrum of everyday existence. So it was like that, the three of us—so unalike and yet the best of friends.

Whew! The mountain run had sort of built up a whopping appetite. I had seen a kiosk, which in local parlance is called a dhaba, where one could sit down on wooden benches and drink hot, thick, and treacle-infused tea accompanied by fruit buns. In the midst of such happy thoughts, all of a sudden, a vision of my angelic-looking Mum manifested itself in between the teacup and my face.

Good Lord! She has grown horns too! came the unwelcome thought. There was nothing angelic about her as she launched into a tirade with a sniff. *I thought I told you not to think about unhealthy food. No one will marry you. All the eligible ones are looking for size 0 these days!*

Grrr! Mum, I am not fat, just well rounded. If one cannot consume gastronomic delights in one's lifetime, then pray, when can one partake of it? The next life? As was expected, the scowl deepened. Ignoring that, I continued, *Is there another life after this, and if not, what will happen to all that we miss out in this, culinary magic included?*

Aditi gave me a hard kick on the shin, saying, 'Don't you ever listen, Rita? I am famished. Come on, let's go and grab a bite. I think I saw an eating joint down the road.'

'Uh-huh! Yes, let's go,' I said.

Surreptitiously, I looked at Aditi as I rose to do her bidding. She seemed to have developed a demonic look in the interregnum. *Temptation, thy name is Satan!*

What the hell? I thought, silently begging the *absent mater* for forgiveness. After all, one had to eat. Angels were not worth a dime when there was a royal repast.

Ramona joined us, wheezing and gulping huge amounts of air. She had the look of a creature that had just gotten off a non-stop twenty-four-hour roller-coaster ride. She was one person who definitely required to be fed to the gills.

The evening shadows lengthened. Out in the hills, darkness set in early and, after that, a heavy luncheon replete with stuffed leavened bread (paratha) with dollops of butter, a side dish of thick yoghurt blended with herbs and spices, and two glasses of thick milky tea. It was accompanied by an old rheumy-eyed man singing old soulful songs and a harassed middle-aged woman, presumably the aged one's daughter, shouting at the cook; it had been a satisfying day.

I had voted for an early night as we had to leave early in the morning and it was a long drive—about twelve hours non-stop—weather, traffic and other preponderant conditions permitting. Aditi and Ramona went off to their rooms, which were adjacent to mine—I had the one between theirs—discussing some herbal beauty treatment and its benefits.

The guest house was really quiet; we were the only occupants that night. We had heard that a large group was coming in the next day all the way from Chennai, which was in the southern part of the country. The guest house management was glad that we were checking out early, for all the twenty rooms had been booked.

After having completed my nightly ritual of calling up the parents, I switched off the light. As what would invariably happened after a hectic day, although I was tired, sleep did not come easily. Initially, I felt warm and even kicked off the coverlet. But in spite of doing so, Hypnos, the blessed god of sleep, continued to elude me. I could hear the grandfather clock go *tick tock, tick tock*, and listening to that, my mind wandered off to the idea of buying a cuckoo clock once I reached home.

Having fixed that thought, I turned around to delve deep into the land of Nod. I could hear the girls giggling in the next room. For a moment, I was tempted to bound out of bed and tumble into their room. But on second thought, I gave up the idea, for we had to get up early and hit the road. If I did not get up, we would surely miss the bus because these two would not surface on their own, and if we did not reach at the appointed time, then there would be hell to pay from the parents.

So I started counting sheep backwards from 600. Anything less than that did not work because I count very fast. And wait, I was not an insomniac. Strange and unfamiliar environs did that to me.

432, 431 . . . 28 . . . 24, 23 . . . zzz.

I did not know when I dropped off to sleep. Something woke me up. I looked out of the window; it was pitch-dark outside. The time was 3.06 a.m. How on earth did I know that? It was dark, and I was not wearing a watch. Quickly, I switched on the bedside lamp. The grandfather clock showed 3.26 a.m. Strange. Why had that specific time flit through my mind then? There was a twenty-minute time lag between that appearing in the dream and the actual time! Was it significant? Maybe it was. I turned over on to my stomach and dropped off to sleep.

Five o' clock in the morning, and I was awake. It was a task waking up the two of them, but threatening to dump them and leave did the trick. We managed to catch the bus by the skin of our teeth. Slowly, the vehicle manoeuvred itself around the hilly bends and curves on its return journey. All seats were occupied, and the music system continued to belt out local beats. Gradually, the chattering passengers started dozing off. The three of us talked for a while, reminiscing about the high points of our holiday.

All of a sudden, there was a screeching of brakes, a thundering sound, and the sound of crunching metal. Then, there was sudden silence all round.

The siren of the ambulance permeated her consciousness. The nurse attending her looked worriedly at the doctor.

'She is sinking,' she said. A policeman said that it would take thirty minutes to clear the road. The doctor said, 'She won't survive beyond twenty minutes.'

600, 599 . . . zzz . . . zzz.

25

Lullaby

Mala woke up each day at 5 a.m. It was immaterial whether she slept at the usual time, which would usually be, as part of routine, at half past ten. Sometimes it was delayed by over an hour if she was waylaid by her whining mother, who invariably always chose the odd hour of ten in the night to narrate her trials and tribulations at the hands of an uncaring son and a vicious daughter-in-law or, for lack of anything better to crib about, to complain about her aching joints and how she was just hanging on to life by a delicate thread.

Such sessions invariably needed to be concluded by popping an aspirin to remove the blinding headache, which followed in its wake. These were not the only causes of a delayed bedtime. Many a time after she had completed all her chores, her beloved husband of three years, Ajit, would want to chat about his day, hers too, and even about their baby, Anuj. Chatting with her husband, however, was always a pleasure, unlike those with her mum.

Anuj, the apple of their eye, was a gurgling and chubby thirteen-month-old baby. He was a happy child—no bawling. He chortled all day while looking happily at the rattle above his crib. Nor did he make any fuss at meal times. In fact, he was no trouble at all. *To add to his numerous positive qualities,* thought the fond mother, *he does not even wake me up most nights.* Even now, he was sleeping just like what he was—a baby.

Her friends all marvelled at how lucky she was—a handsome and caring husband, a beautiful child, and a house which ran like a well-oiled machine. Of course, according to Ajit, the credit went to her; her husband was generous and fulsome in his praise of her before anyone who cared to listen. She very efficiently handled all the aspects of her home—the grocery, the interior, the cook, the maid, the driver, and the gardener. As a hands-on mother, she looked after all of Anuj's needs herself. None of the help was allowed to touch him. She bathed him, clothed him, fed him, and put him to bed all by herself.

So she was up at 5 a.m. again as usual. Ajit was asleep, so she pottered around the kitchen, fixing a cup of tea for herself. She put the kettle on to boil and went to the patio to look for the faint stirrings of dawn. No such luck, not even the sound of birds. *I'm up before the proverbial lark,* she thought wryly.

Stretching one final time, she went back to the kitchen, and pouring out her tea into a cup, she picked it up along with a couple of biscuits and made her way to the lounge, where she would sip her tea, waiting for morning to make an appearance.

The morning flew by in a whirl. It was 11 a.m. Ajit had left for the office, the dishes had been cleared away, the washed clothes hung out to dry, and all was well with the world. Now was the time to check up on Anuj, for it was feeding time.

*   *   *

Tring, tring.

'Pick up the phone, Ajit!'

'Hello, Mala, I am in a meeting. I shall call you later.' Saying this, Ajit was about to disconnect when he realized that the voice which spoke from the caller's end was not Mala. The voice carried through on an urgent note, 'Mr Ajit, I am Dr Sinha. Please come to Shreya Hospital immediately.'

'What happened? Where's Mala?' asked Ajit, striving to keep the panic out of his voice.

'Sir, just come over right now,' said the doctor, disconnecting abruptly.

Hospitals, all of them are the same, he thought. They were sanitized, yet in that cleanliness always lingered the strange smell of disinfectant. He had always hated them. He went to the reception and was given directions to Dr Sinha's room. He knocked on his door. A voice bade him to come in. Entering, he saw a white coat–clad doctor come up to him and lead him to a seat.

After he sat down, the doctor said, 'I am sorry to be the one who has to say this. It's your wife, Mr Ajit. She brought in your son after smothering him. She had been torturing him for a long time. There are numerous scars and marks of old wounds on his body. She probably hurt him when there was no one at home so that no one would have heard his cries of pain. She had also been giving him sedatives at night so that he would not disturb her.'

Ajit screamed, but it was a wordless one as tears streamed down his face. In the ground behind the doctor's chamber, a cat licked her litter of kittens.

About the Author

Mona Mohanty has had a passion for short stories since childhood. She has served as an officer of the Indian Revenue Service for more than two decades and currently lives in New Delhi.

Printed in the United States
By Bookmasters